FALLEN STAR

DEBRA CLAYTON

URBAN BOOKS LLC
www.urbanbooks.net

Urban Books
74 Andrews Avenue
Wheatley Heights, NY 11798

ISBN 1-893196-42-9

First Printing May 2006
Printed in the United States of America

10 9 8 7 6 5 4 3 2 1

This is a work of fiction. Any references or similarities to actual events, real people, living, or dead, or to real locales are intended to give the novel a sense of reality. Any similarity in other names, characters, places, and incidents is entirely coincidental.

Submit Wholesale Orders to:
Kensington Publishing Corp.
c/o Penguin Group (USA) Inc.
Attention: Order Processing
405 Murray Hill Parkway
East Rutherford, NJ 07073-2316
Phone: 1-800-526-0275
Fax: 1-800-227-9604

FALLEN STAR

Also by Debra Clayton

Rap Superstar

DEDICATIONS

This book is dedicated to my three children, Alexander,
Jennifer and Alicia, without whom,
I wouldn't have a reason to rise in the morning.

ACKNOWLEDGMENTS

I want to say thanks to all the people who were an asset in helping my literary dreams come to fruition. First I want to thank my kids, Alexander, Jennifer and Alicia. Thanks for your patience and understanding and thanks for telling your friends that your mother is a real author. It's nice to know that you are proud of me. Secondly, I want to thank my mother, Jeanella Clayton, who taught me never to give up, whose trashy novels and *True Story* magazines were the foundation for my writing career and for your strengths. Thank you for fighting the good fight, going against the odds, and showing me that no matter how high I get, I'm never too high to get down on my knees and look up. You are my hero. Thirdly, I want to thank my sisters Jean Hines and Octavia Clayton for being wonderful sisters. Thanks for the insight that you offer when I'm working on one of my masterpieces and thanks for listening as I go on and on about new stories and new ideas. I also want to thank Toni Adams. I should include you as one of my sisters because you are one to me. I pray that you will continue to enjoy my stories and that I will continue to fuel your hunger for them. Next, I want to say thanks to my mother-in-law. Even though your son and I didn't last, I'm happy that you and I did. Thanks for always being a friend despite the circumstances. The next person I want to thank is Kathy Brown. Though we do not work together anymore, I still consider you a friend. You have no idea what your friendship means to me and though I may not see you anymore, you are never far from my heart and thoughts. You are still my biggest cheerleader.

I also want to thank Carl Weber. Thanks for taking a chance on me and "Rap Superstar". Thanks for believing that I have to skills to be a part of the Urban Books family. Thanks goes to you too Roy Glenn for always giving me a kind word and a friendly smile.

Finally I want to thank is Steve Pruitt. Thanks for your patience, your love and your attentiveness. Thanks for helping out with the kids, for being my sounding board and thanks for loving me in spite of my wicked ways. Thanks for acknowledging my temper tantrums when I don't get my way and thanks for being strong enough to wait for me while I try to get it together. And thanks be to God, for without Him, I am nothing, without His strength, I can not stand and without His grace, I would not be here today.

Chapter One

"*Slow down, I just want to get to know you*," sang thirty-two-year-old Ethan Michaels as he nodded his head to Bobby Valentino's hit single, "Slow Down." He tapped his fingers lightly on the steering wheel to the beat as he pulled his car into the circular driveway in front of the 6.8 million-dollar European-style mansion. The thirty-five rooms, four-car garage, luxurious home was detailed with sculptured ten-foot ceilings, exquisite millwork, hand-carved columns, and imported solid doors. Sitting on over three acres of land, the ten-bedroom, eleven-bath residence also boasted a wine cellar, an Olympic-size swimming pool in the courtyard, and a full-size basketball court.

But the professionally landscaped lawn and lavish home wasn't Ethan's. The impressive estate belonged to his client, twenty-four-year-old rap sensation, Blayze, aka Calvin Wallace. Also referred to as Atlanta's answer to 50 Cent, Calvin was the newest "rhyme master" coming out of the heart of the South, and Ethan had been his manager for the last two years.

Southern Scope Records contacted Ethan and offered him the job. He'd had a chance to listen to Calvin's demo a few months earlier and knew right away that the rap hopeful was a lyrical genius. Knowing Calvin's potential, Ethan immediately accepted the position.

Not long after becoming his manager, he realized that Calvin was also one of the biggest assholes he'd ever met. But he didn't mind working for an asshole . . . as long as it paid the bills. And from the amount of chips that Calvin was stacking, Ethan had no problem paying the mortgage on the more modest, but spacious, 3,500 square-foot condominium he called home.

After pulling the key out of the ignition, he reached over, picked up the airline ticket and itinerary, and then climbed out of the white gold crystal Lexus SC. He hurried up the steps to the massive home and rang the doorbell.

As he waited for someone to answer the door, he tucked the papers under his arm and pulled out his BlackBerry organizer. He checked his schedule for the next day and noted an appointment to meet with Tymeless Jewelry Company. Tymeless was interested in getting Calvin to endorse their new line of diamond-encrusted watches, which they'd recently designed for highly visible and influential individuals in the hip-hop industry. Witnessing the massive record sales of Calvin's debut CD, Tymeless was convinced that he was on his way to becoming very influential in the hip-hop nation.

But Tymeless wasn't the only business to notice Calvin's potential—he'd already signed contracts to endorse tennis shoes for G-Phorce Shoes, cellular phones for En-Touch Mobile Phone Company, and a new drink called Hype Energy Drink for D & C Beverage Company. One of the most highly sought after rappers out there, Calvin's schedule kept Ethan jumping. But Ethan didn't mind Calvin's popularity, as long as the checks kept rolling in.

After the meeting with Tymeless Jewelry, he would catch his flight to Detroit to meet up with Calvin before his first performance.

"Ethan." Twenty-two-year-old Toni Wallace smiled when she opened the door. "Hi, how are you?"

Toni and Calvin had been married for three years, and although she was his client's wife, Ethan was immediately drawn to her from the first time he met her two years ago. But his attraction to her wasn't for the obvious reasons. She was beautiful. He couldn't deny that. Nor could he deny that she possessed the kind of body that could bring any man, straight or gay, black or white, to his knees. But what attracted him to Toni was her genuine heart.

In the world of hip-hop where most of the beautiful women had either fake hair, fake boobs, fake attitudes, or any combination of each, Toni was real, and she kept it real. Ethan often referred to the other women in the hip-hop world as CZ's, short for cubic zirconia, because they weren't the real thing, but he knew that Toni was a "diamond." When he was first introduced to Calvin, he pictured him being married to some gold-digging princess, but in reality, Calvin had managed to snag himself the ultimate woman. It was just a shame that he treated her like shit.

"Hey, Toni." Ethan attempted to sound casual and unaffected by the magnet that drew him to her. "I'm fine, and you."

"I'm doing great," she nodded. "Come on inside." She stepped back so he could enter.

"No, no." He shook his head and reached up under his arm to get the papers that he had for her husband. "I was just bringing Calvin's airline ticket and itinerary by. I know he had a photo shoot with *Flow* magazine earlier today, but I didn't know what time they would be finished with him. Is he here?"

"No, he hasn't come home yet. Come on inside," she insisted; "I want you to taste something for me."

"I really should—"

"Please . . . it'll only take a second."

"Okay." Ethan stepped inside.

"Thanks. Follow me." She led him into the kitchen. The spacious gourmet-style kitchen was so well equipped with the finest state-of-the-art appliances and accessories; it would've made even the most finicky chef swoon. And although Toni didn't consider herself much of a cook, Calvin's insistence that intricately carved cabinetry and woodwork accent the already stunning cooking area made the little time she spent in the kitchen almost heavenly.

"I've made this surprise dinner for Calvin," she explained. "Sort of a going-away dinner since his tour starts tomorrow. Could you taste this meatloaf and let me know what you think. He loves meatloaf. I tried to make it the way his mother did." She cut off a piece of the meatloaf and fed it to him.

Ethan closed his eyes and savored the flavor. "Mmmm, this is delicious." He opened his eyes up and looked down at her. He smiled. "You did your thing, woman."

4

"Really? You like it, or are you bullshitting me?"

"I love it. I wish Kenya could cook like you."

"Kenya? Who's Kenya?"

Toni put the fork down, folded her arms, leaned on the counter, and stared up at him. Her eyes strolled over the smooth, hazel-brown skin of his face as she studied his strong jaw line, full velvet lips, and dark, yet warm eyes. *Damn, he is fine.* She wondered what it would feel like to kiss those strong, velvet lips of his, which seemed so inviting. She wondered what kind of woman it would take to steal his heart.

Although she felt a spiritual connection with Ethan and couldn't deny a physical attraction to him, she was never one to step out on her husband. And even though he worked for her husband, Ethan had proven to be a good friend to her. In time she had come to rely on him and his friendship. Whenever Calvin's antics got the better of her and she needed a nonjudgmental shoulder to lean on, Ethan was always more than willing to lend his. She hoped that the woman to capture his heart would be able to appreciate his gentle kindness and giving soul. She also hoped that his new lady wouldn't put an end to their unique and special friendship.

"Oh, she's just a lady that I've been seeing for a couple of months."

"Really," she smiled with intrigue. "Calvin never mentioned that you had a girlfriend." Suddenly she was feeling a little envious of Kenya. She wondered what it would be like to be Ethan's woman and to have his soft patient hands on her body as he made love to her instead of being fucked as usual by her husband. She was sure that Ethan, unlike her husband, was a gentle lover. It was just too bad that she was a married and faithful woman.

"Well, I don't know if I would call her a girlfriend." Ethan didn't want to give her the impression that he was taken or unavailable just in case she came to her senses and decided to leave her philandering husband. Ethan wasn't one to break up a happy home, but from where he sat, the Wallace's home wasn't a happy one.

"So what is she then?—A booty call?" Toni knew that Ethan was too much of a gentleman to refer to a woman as a booty call.

"No, not a booty call." He chuckled. "She's just someone I kick it with every now and then; she's good people."

"Well, whatever you call her, I'm glad you found someone. You need a good woman in your life; you deserve it." She smiled as she stopped leaning on the counter and stood straight up.

"Thanks."

"No problem."

As he stared down at Toni, he wondered where Calvin was. *He is probably somewhere with his dick shoved down some chick's throat.* He remembered the incident that occurred a little less than two years ago. He caught Calvin in the recording studio with his pants down around his ankles, fucking some girl that he'd only been introduced to a couple of hours earlier. It was then he realized that Calvin was a "grade-A" asshole. The worst part was Toni knew he was unfaithful. He was blatant with the shit that he did. And even though Ethan knew Calvin's infidelities hurt her, for some reason she remained steadfast by her husband's side. Ethan didn't know why a beautiful woman like Toni subjected herself to such abuse and disrespect. *How could she not know?* He could only attribute it to her being foolishly in love. Most sistas he knew would have cut Calvin's dick off and flushed it down the toilet by now if he'd treated them the way he treated Toni.

Instead, Toni was cooking him a fantastic going-away dinner. Ethan just didn't get it.

"Listen, Toni, I've got to get going. Could you make sure Calvin gets these?" He handed her the papers. "And tell him I'll see him tomorrow in Detroit."

"Okay." Toni took the papers and walked him to the door. "You be careful and have a safe trip."

"Thanks. I will."

"And please look after my husband. Even though he tries to be tough, he's really nervous about giving his first big concert."

"I'll try, Toni, but you know Calvin." Ethan laughed.

"All too well." She smiled.

After he left, Toni busied herself in the kitchen, putting the final touches on her meal. She glanced at her watch. It was six o'clock. She wasn't sure what time her husband would be arriving home, but she thought about hurrying since he could walk through the door any minute. She wanted to make sure the dining room was completely set up for his going-away dinner. Tonight was going to be special in more ways than one, and she didn't want anything to mess it up, including him.

"Don't blow it, Calvin," she mumbled under her breath as she remembered all the other times he had disappointed her. "Not tonight. I have too many plans for us tonight, baby."

Chapter Two

Hours later, across town, it was obvious that Toni's husband had other plans for his last night in town. The up-and-coming rap star had made his way to a local club and was sitting back, enjoying the trappings of his newfound success. Although people were just finding out who he was and often referred to him as an overnight celebrity, he knew all too well that his new status in the hip-hop world didn't come overnight, but took years.

Before practically spending a year and a half living in the studio as he worked on his CD with producers Iceman and Fat Boy, he'd spent two years on the streets of Atlanta, trying to get his demo into the right hands. Prior to that, he'd spent three years, with the help of his girlfriend, now wife, Toni, perfecting his craft.

Toni was the reason he'd even considered a career in the hip-hop industry. After reading some of his poetry, she encouraged him to try rapping and became his biggest cheerleader. He knew he owed all of his success to her even though he treated her like shit.

He thought about the phone call he had received from his manager three hours earlier. "Triple platinum," Ethan said when he informed Calvin just how well his sales were going on his debut CD, "Priceless." And this was only three months after Southern Scope Records released the CD.

"Three months," Calvin said to himself, "and I'm blowing up already." He raised his glass to an imaginary toast. "This is for all the mean-mugging muthafuckas who said I wouldn't amount to shit—you all can kiss my pretty black ass." He chuckled and then took a sip of his drink.

He thought about all the haters who said he wouldn't make it. He didn't roll with an entourage; he didn't need one. He didn't need a bunch of wannabe niggas trying to hitch their wagons to his star. When he was trying to come up and asked other brothas for a hand, they just mocked him. Now those same niggas wanted to roll with him. He didn't have time for fake-ass friends.

The only real friend he had was David Moore, a fellow label mate. They were both signed to Southern Scope Records and, according to the media, were supposed to be competing against each other. Instead, they forged a friendship. David was actually supposed to be out helping him celebrate tonight, but his mean-ass wife, Traci, wouldn't let him off the chain that she'd wrapped around his neck.

As he watched the talent on the dance floor below the VIP room, he nodded his head to the beat of 50 Cent's "Just a Lil' Bit."

He thought about where he was a little over two years ago. At age twenty-two, armed with a demo and a "don't-take-no-for-an-answer" attitude, he was pounding the streets of Atlanta, looking for an opportunity to slip his demo into the right hands. He was hanging out at clubs like this one, hoping to get just close enough to one of the industry's heavyweights so he could slip one of them a sample of what he could do.

Most of the time when he was noticed loitering around the clubs or trying to get next to the top-notch hip-hop producers; security would kick him out on his pretty black ass. Frustrated and tired, he often felt like giving up, but with his new wife at home encouraging him to keep on keeping on, he found the energy and the will to hit the streets again the next day.

His persistence finally paid off. One night, while hanging around the entrance of the VIP lounge of the same upscale club he was lounging in now, The Next Episode, he managed to slip into the VIP room where hip-hop producer, Iceman, was chilling.

In the short ten years that he had been producing tracks for hip-hop artists, Iceman had become a legend. He had a knack for turning unknown wannabe rappers into rap superstars. He was the one to work with if you wanted to make a splash in the industry. Due to lax security, he was able to slip into the VIP room and get close enough to Iceman to give him his demo.

"One track," Calvin begged as he shoved the demo into Iceman's hand. "Just listen to one track."

But as quickly as he slipped into the VIP room, he was snatched up by security and tossed out again.

Three weeks later, Southern Scope Records, a mid-size record company in the heart of Atlanta, contacted Calvin about getting him into the studio. Shortly after impressing the executives at the record company, he signed a deal with them.

Two years later, he was sitting in the VIP room at the same club security kicked him out of, getting his drink on as he prepared himself to start his three-month tour.

His tour would start the following day in Detroit and end three months later in Houston. The sixty-city tour excited him as he thought about all the fans who purchased his debut CD. He also thought about all the beautiful women that he could get into while on the road.

Although married for the past three years, Calvin didn't let that stop him from sampling ladies at the pussy buffet. Yeah, *I am the shit now.* He sipped on his glass of Hennessy and signaled for one of the bouncers to come over.

As he continued watching the talent on the dance floor through the glass partition separating him from the rest of the club, he spotted a young woman that sparked more than his interest. Just watching her shake her ass on the dance floor made his dick rock-hard. The way she was bouncing and jiggling her ass off of the brotha she was dancing with made him think of the way she would feel bouncing her ass off of him while he fucked her from behind.

He smiled at the thought of blowing her back out. Toni would never let him fuck her like that. But she wasn't Toni. She was just some chick whose pussy he wanted to beat up. He figured he'd get her up in the VIP room, see how long it took to get her panties off, and fuck the hell outta her. Later he'd go home and get a second nut with his wife. He'd give her a going-away fuck so she'd have something to remember him by while he was on tour.

"Yes, sir, Mr. Wallace," the bouncer said as he approached him.

"See the redbone in the black mini that's driving those niggas crazy down there? Invite her upstairs."

"Yes, sir."

As he watched the bouncer summon the girl, he heard a loud commotion outside the door of the VIP room. Calvin looked over to see what was happening. Dollar Bill, the former reigning king of rap, along with two of his boys, were quickly ushered into the room as they fought off screaming fans. Although Dollar Bill had slipped into the club via the back door to avoid causing a scene, a few fans spotted him and rushed him at the VIP room entrance.

Calvin watched as Dollar Bill hastily autographed a woman's cleavage just before security pushed the patrons back outside of the room and closed the door.

"You gotta love 'em," Dollar Bill said to one of his boys. "It's fans like that that make you number one." He straightened up his suit and walked over to the sofa to sit down.

Smiling to himself, Calvin strolled over to meet him. "Number two," he said.

"Number two?" Dollar Bill twisted his mouth disapprovingly. "And who the hell are you?"

"You ought to know who I am." Calvin smiled. "I'm the nigga that took your number one spot."

Dollar Bill looked him up and down and still wasn't impressed. *So this was the little son of a bitch that had knocked him down to number two.*

For the last five years Dollar Bill was consistently knocking wannabe MC's on their asses when they came up against him. Even though his stage name was Dollar Bill, the media had dubbed him King Midas because everything he touched turned to gold. He was spitting out shitloads of number one hits that drove the competition back from where they came. That was until Blayze stepped on the scene and demanded to have the spotlight turned on him. He was the first and only MC to knock Dollar Bill off his throne.

Dollar Bill wasn't feeling this young kid, whose ambition was to steal his title. "No disrespect, young buck, but you're a short-timer—you don't have what it takes to stay at the top, so enjoy it while you're there. Take plenty of pictures because next week it'll only be a memory." Dollar Bill grinned, showing his mouthful of gold teeth.

"I'll tell you what I'll do, old man—I'll take pictures and send them to you so you'll be able to remember what it used to be like before I got here. You see, I ain't going nowhere. Get used to looking up at me 'cause I'm staying on top. Now if you don't mind"—he looked over at the young lady he had sent for as she walked toward him—"I'm gonna help myself to the pussy buffet." With that, he left to meet his guest.

The beauty was even more stunning than he thought. "I'm Blayze." He smiled as he introduced himself.

"I know." She was unable to hide her excitement. "I'm Layla."

"Well, I'm glad you could join me, Layla." He directed her to the sofa. "Would you like a drink?" His eyes roamed over the spectacular view she provided.

"Yes," she answered as she sat down.

Just as he was about to signal the waitress, his cell phone rang. He quickly pulled out his phone and glanced at the caller ID. It was his wife, Toni. This was the ninth call from her. He decided to take it. "Just a second," he said to Layla and answered the call. "Hello."

"Calvin, it's one o'clock in the morning. When are you coming home?"

"I'll be there when I get there, baby. You know I leave out tomorrow. I'm just trying to celebrate my last night in town before I go on the road."

"I know. That's why I'm calling. I thought you would spend your last night in town with me. I cooked dinner and everything."

"Well, keep it warm for me, Toni."

"Keep it warm for you? Dinner was at seven o'clock. It's now one in the morning. I've been calling you and waiting for you all night, and all you can say is keep it warm for you." She was so tired of his bullshit, of him fucking around. All she needed was one night from him, and he wouldn't even give her that.

"Damn it, Toni, stop riding me. I'll be home in a minute, but right now I've gotta go. I've got some fans waiting for me." He hung up the phone without waiting for a response.

"Who was that?" Layla asked.

"Just my wife."

She raised an eyebrow. "Your wife?"

"That's not a problem, is it?"

"Not for me." She smiled.

"Good. Now let's get you a drink and get this shit popping." He laughed as he signaled the waitress.

After ordering a bottle of Cristal, he turned his attention back to Layla. "I was watching you on the dance floor downstairs and I like the way you shake your ass, baby girl."

"Oh really?" she smiled. "Well, since I'm up here with you now, maybe you can watch me do it up close and personal."

"Hell, yeah. I don't have problem with that. Go ahead and do your thing, girl."

Layla, who never considered herself the shy type, stood up and started rotating her hips in a manner that ass-jiggled just the way he liked it.

"Damn, girl, I like the way you work that." Calvin stood up and moved behind her. He grabbed her hips and pulled her closer.

Without missing a beat, she continued working her ass on him as he began to grind his already hard dick between her cheeks.

"I like the way you roll, baby girl," he whispered in her ear.

She laughed. "Well, you know, ain't no shame in my game."

Almost on the verge of tears, Toni slammed down the receiver, jumped out of bed, and raced downstairs and into the kitchen. She glared at the dirty pots and pans that filled the kitchen sink as she hurried into the exquisitely decorated dining room. The intricately carved woodwork on the built-in wall units matched the carvings found on the equally stunning fireplace and decorative columns. Along the soft amber-colored walls were large bay windows accented with rich Merlot Jacquard, pinch-pleated draperies. The thick, hand-sewn drapes were pulled opened, allowing sunlight to dance across the hardwood floors during the daytime and the soft glow of the moonlight to spill into the room at night. The elaborately carved, double-pedestal, French provincial dining room table was still set for two with fine china and a fresh bouquet of flowers cut from the courtyard garden and arranged into a delicate centerpiece.

She stood there looking over the meatloaf, mash potatoes, greens, and homemade biscuits that she had slaved over earlier. Anger welled up inside her. *All for nothing,* she thought. She walked over to the table, picked up the plate of cold food, and threw it against the wall. She watched as the plate shattered and the food slid down the wall and fell onto the hardwood floor.

"You sorry piece of shit." She picked up her plate and threw it at the dining room window, causing the contents to cover the expensive drapes. "I hate you," she screamed. She knew why he wasn't home—he was somewhere fucking one of his groupies. She was tired of being treated like shit, of him taking her for granted and assuming she would always be there because of the prenuptial agreement. The prenup that she'd signed when she was too foolishly in love to know any better, when she thought they'd be together forever.

"Fuck that prenup." Toni burst into tears and began grabbing anything that was within her reach and throwing it across the room. *It would all be over soon.* All of his infidelities and total disrespect for her would all be over when her plan was complete. Soon she would be gone. She'd pack up the little bit of shit that she accumulated in their marriage and walk out of his life for good. *Fuck Calvin, fuck his prenuptial agreement, and fuck this entire marriage.* Tears raced down her face, blurring her vision, as she destroyed their dining room and vowed to put an end to her pain forever.

Across town, in the back of his black pimped-out H2, Calvin was deep inside Layla's pussy.

"Oh shit," she cried out as he fucked her deep and hard from behind. The glow from the streetlight gave him just enough light to enjoy the view, and the sight of her ass jiggling as it bounced off him made him want to blow her back out.

"What's my name?" He watched the wet juices of her pussy coat his shaft with each stroke.

"Blayze," she moaned.

"What's my name?" he asked her again.

"Blayze," she said a little louder as she looked over her shoulder and watched him.

His entire body was rock-hard as sweat raced down his straining muscles. "Bitch, what's my name?"

"Blayze," she cried out. Layla dropped her head and tried to deal with the pain of him trying to fuck her brains out.

"Say my muthafuckin' name!" he yelled.

"Blayze!" she screamed. "Blayze! Blayze! Oh God, you're hurting me. Please, slow down." She tried to pull away from him.

Ignoring her pleas, he gripped her hips to hold her still and fuck her even harder. "Not yet, baby. I'm about to cum. I'm about to cum, muthafucka," he growled.

Layla squeezed her eyes closed and gritted her teeth as she waited for him to finish.

Seconds later, Calvin rammed himself deep inside her and shot his load. "Oh shit, I'm cumming."

Once Layla felt his grip on her loosen, she began to relax. She slipped away from him, turned around, and watched him.

Calvin remained on his knees, stared up at the roof of the car, and basked in the afterglow of his nut.

Layla smiled when she saw this.

Feeling her gaze, he looked down at her. "You like that, baby?" He slipped his condom off, rolled down the window, and tossed it outside in the parking lot.

"Yeah, Blayze. I loved the way you fucked me."

Even though he nearly fucked the hell out of her, she had a story to go back and tell all of her friends—she fucked Blayze—rap superstar, Blayze.

An hour later, Calvin climbed into the bed with Toni. The weight of her husband's body awakened her. Still angry, she rolled over on her side and put her back to him.

He knew she was pissed. "Toni," he whispered. He slid up behind her and pulled her against him.

She didn't respond.

"Toni." He kissed her neck. "I'm sorry, baby; I lost track of time."

She turned over and faced him. "I deserve better than this, Calvin."

He could hear the hurt in her voice. "I'm sorry, baby. I know." He kissed her lips as his hands traveled over her body and pulled at her lingerie to make his intentions clear.

Toni pushed him away. "You sick bastard!" she hissed. "You didn't even have the decency to wash the pussy off your face before climbing in the bed with me."

He rolled over and climbed out of bed. "Bitch, I just went triple platinum; you should feel privileged that I still want to fuck you. And if you don't like the taste of pussy, then get the hell out. You know where the door is." He went to the bedroom door and grabbed the doorknob.

"Calvin, no . . . please." She jumped out of bed and hur-

19

ried over to him. "I'm sorry." She was on the verge of tears as she pulled his face down and began kissing. "I'm sorry, baby. Don't leave."

He released the doorknob and grabbed her. He slammed his mouth down on top of hers and kissed her hard, hurting her lips. Then he slid his hands down to her buttocks, picked her up, wrapped her legs around his waist, and carried her back to the bed. He quickly tore at her clothes until she lay naked before him.

She stared up at him.

He looked like a wild boar as he pushed her legs apart and buried his face in her womanhood. Savagely, he licked, sucked, and probed her with his tongue until she climaxed against her will.

Damn. She cursed herself as she felt her body betray her.

He quickly climbed on top of her and rammed himself inside her repeatedly. Toni closed her eyes and cried softly from the humiliation.

He continued to plow himself inside her until he climaxed. In one quick motion, he rolled off her, climbed out of bed, and went into the bathroom to dispose of the condom. Without a word to his wife, he quickly returned to bed and turned his back to her.

Still sobbing quietly, Toni climbed out of bed and retreated to the bathroom, where she locked the door. She ran some bathwater and thought about the last seven years. *It wasn't always like this.* He used to treat her like he loved her, but since the record deal from Southern Scope Records a lot had changed.

* * *

She wished she could brag about marrying her high-school sweetheart, but there was nothing to brag about. Toni and Calvin met when she was fifteen and he was seventeen. He'd moved into her neighborhood with his single mother. (His father had taken off when he was only two years old.) Toni shared the same type of abandonment, but her father had left before she was even born. Both being the only child from a single-parent home, they understood each other and immediately clicked upon their first meeting. When she first saw the handsome seventeen-year-old moving into the house next door, she immediately developed a crush on him. She didn't know, however, that four months later he would take her virginity in the back seat of his Ford Escort.

From that moment on, Toni thought she and Calvin would be together forever. He treated her like a queen, and they were inseparable.

A couple of years later, Calvin dropped to one knee and asked Toni to marry him. She was surprised, however, that he asked her to sign a prenuptial agreement. Little did she know, that little piece of paper would come back to bite her in the ass.

She turned off the bathwater, turned on the jets, and climbed into the AirMasseur Therapy bathtub. As she slid down into the bath, the water temperature was a little higher than she expected, and the heat made her cringe. But as her body quickly adjusted to the temperature, she began to relax.

Her mind returned to her husband, snoring lightly in the next room. The first year of their marriage was what she termed "a sweet struggle." Shortly after saying their "I do's," Toni and Calvin moved into a small apartment on the poorer side of Atlanta. And even though she was awarded a full scholarship to go to Wake Forest University in North Carolina, she gave it up so she could go to work and help with the household bills and expenses that came with Calvin's dream of becoming a rapper. Studio time and demos were not cheap, and they needed every cent they could get. So she and Calvin both held down full-time jobs.

Toni worked at a local restaurant as a waitress, while Calvin delivered packages for UPS. Then, they spent little time together in the evenings. Toni would either spend her evenings curled up reading romance novels or watching detective dramas on TV, while Calvin spent his evenings hanging out in nightclubs, trying to get next to the heavyweights of the hip-hop industry. His goal was to get his demo into the right hands.

Toni didn't mind spending her evenings alone. She knew they had to make sacrifices to make his dreams come to fruition. When Calvin finally made it home to her, if he wasn't beaten down by the streets, he would make love to her all night long. If the streets had broken his spirit and he wanted to give up on his dream, she would spend the nights repairing the damage that the streets had done by reminding him just how gifted he was and encouraging him to keep on keeping on. She pleaded for him not to give up because the opportunity that he was looking for could be just around the next corner. After successfully picking his spirits up, they would resume their normal lovemaking. Life was good back then.

A few weeks after celebrating their one-year anniversary,

Calvin got the break he was looking for. He managed to get his demo to Iceman. Shortly after that, he had a record deal. It was after he signed the deal with Southern Scope Records that Toni started noticing changes in her husband's behavior. Their marathon lovemaking sessions became less frequent. In fact, some nights he never even made it home.

"We were working on the CD all night long," he sometimes claimed.

She believed him in the beginning, but when he started coming home the next morning smelling like other women's perfume, she became suspicious. Later, provocative photos of him with other women surfaced in the tabloids and confirmed her suspicions.

At first, Calvin denied that the photos were authentic, but as tabloids published more pictures, he admitted to cheating, saying, "These women mean nothing to me," he said; "they're just a little something on the side."

Toni informed him that she wasn't going to play second string to his ho's and threatened to leave him if he didn't stop screwing around. He promised her that all of his running around was over, that he was going to be faithful.

Later, when more evidence of his infidelities surfaced, she again threatened to leave. His response that time was, "If you leave me, you ain't getting shit. Why you think I had you sign that prenup?"

She couldn't believe he'd throw the agreement in her face after all she'd done to help him to get to where he was now. At that moment, Toni realized that Calvin was no longer the man that she had married; he was a stranger to her. He was now a product of the hip-hop industry, created from the fast fame, fast money, and fast women. She was sickened by the idea he would stoop so low and was determined not to walk away from her marriage empty-handed. *I put too much time and love in, helping him develop his career, to end up with nothing.*"

As Calvin's career grew, so did his ego and his infidelities. He became blatant about his running around and no longer tried to hide it from her. Everybody knew he was screwing around. Her mother knew, his mother knew, and their friends knew. And although they tried not to get involved, they made it clear to him that they were disappointed in him.

Embarrassed by her husband's actions, she began to pull away from her friends and family and kept to herself. Finally, unable to accept his behavior anymore, she devised a way to walk away from their marriage and still get paid.

She decided to get pregnant; that way, she could get child support from him. Child support was nothing compared to the fifty percent she felt he owed her, but she also knew that it was nothing to sneeze at. From the amount of dollars that Calvin was pulling in, she knew those child support checks would still be very generous and would help her maintain the lifestyle she'd become accustomed to.

When she told her husband that she thought that they were ready start having kids, he became very suspicious of her intentions. He'd heard so many stories of gold-digging women getting pregnant "to get at a brotha's cheddar." He prided himself on being nobody's fool—not even his wife's.

As soon as he realized what she was up to, he started wearing condoms. He wouldn't touch her without wearing one, except if she was performing oral sex on him, throwing an unexpected wrench into her plan to gain financial freedom from him.

But Toni was undaunted. She still had one more idea that she wanted to put into motion before submitting to her husband's ultimatum of either staying and dealing with his running around or leaving empty-handed. She had no intention of doing either, and if things went as planned, she'd get her share of his millions, even if it meant settling for less than the half that she felt she was entitled to. Two years of being treated like shit was all she was going to take.

She slid down into the water and allowed it to rise up to her neck. He owed her, and if he wasn't going to give it to her, she'd take what she deserved.

Chapter Three

The next morning when Toni awoke, she looked over at her husband. He was still asleep. It was only when he slept that she knew he could be trusted. If he were awake, she knew he'd be out fucking some chick whose name he probably didn't even know. *Soon it would be over,* she thought, *and I would be able to walk out of his life forever without being empty-handed.*

The night before, the argument about him not coming home had spoiled her plan to get what she needed from him. But this morning, she was going to do whatever it took to get what she needed. She smiled to herself as she reached over and groped his semi-erect manhood.

He stirred a little at her touch but didn't wake.

She pulled the covers back, revealing his nakedness, slid over next to him, and began to stroke him. "Baby," she whispered. She slipped her tongue into his ear.

Calvin smiled as he began to recognize her touch. Without opening his eyes, he reached over and grabbed a handful of ass.

"I'm gonna take care of you this morning, baby." Her mouth began to journey south.

He opened his eyes and looked down at her as she traced her tongue around his nipple, causing them to become erect.

"Don't you worry about a thing." She paused to look up at him. "Toni's gonna take care of you real good. Gonna send you off the right way. The only way a woman should send her man." She kissed his stomach as she moved lower.

"You do that, girl." He moaned when he felt the warm wetness of her mouth envelope his manhood.

Although Toni's only sexual experience had been with Calvin, she knew how to please him, and she definitely knew how to use her mouth to blow his mind. She knew how because he'd taught her. He told her everything to do to get him off, and she was more than willing to do whatever it took to satisfy him. And although he had fucked many experienced women since his first time with Toni, no one could put it on him like she could.

Calvin watched her intensely as she used her skillful mouth and tongue to bring him indescribable pleasure. He pushed his hips up to meet her every stroke. "Damn, Toni," he moaned as he felt his passion mount.

She smiled inwardly, knowing that she was driving him crazy. When his breathing began to come hard and fast, she knew it was almost time.

He put his hand on the back of her head and encouraged her to take more of him as he began pumping himself deeper in her mouth.

She continued to nurse on him, trying not to gag.

Although the head of his penis was already stroking the entrance of her throat, Calvin knew better than to go any further. Toni put up with a lot of shit from him, but she wasn't going to deep throat him.

"Oh shit, Toni. I'm gonna cum, baby. I'm gonna cum all in your mouth." He began fucking her mouth wildly.

Go ahead, baby, Toni thought as she continued working on him. *Give it to me. Give it all to me.*

"Muthafucka," he cried out as he plowed himself deep inside her mouth and exploded.

Toni sucked up all the warm juices that spilled into her mouth and made sure not to swallow. She never swallowed, but this time she had a reason not to. She had special plans for his semen today. Once his manhood went limp in her mouth, she released it and climbed out of bed. She hurried into the bathroom, and instead of spitting the semen into the toilet like she normally did, this time she spit it into a plastic cup, placed a lid on it, and hid it under the bathroom sink. She would take care of it later after her husband left.

Before returning to the bedroom, she started the shower for him. "Now you have something to remember me by," she said, re-entering their bedroom. She smiled. Now she had what she needed to make her plan work.

Calvin sat up in the bed, watched her and chuckled. "I always have something to remember you by."

"Your shower's running." She handed him a fresh towel and washcloth from the linen closet.

"Thanks, babe." She was beautiful, he thought. Everything was beautiful about her, from the jet-black, silky curls that spilled down over her shoulder, to her angelic face, to her fabulous figure, to her perfectly manicured fingers and toes. He knew she could do better; he knew she deserved better. But he also knew that she wasn't going anywhere.

He knew Toni loved him, but he knew it wasn't her love for him that kept her from leaving him. It was the prenuptial agreement that he got her to sign. He often wondered why she'd agreed to such an outrageous request. But her reasons didn't matter any more—she had signed the papers, and there was nothing she could do about it now.

He remembered when she started talking about them having kids. He knew what she was up to. He knew that if she got pregnant then she could leave him and demand child support. That's when he started wearing condoms. He knew that as long as he had the prenuptial agreement and she never got pregnant, she wouldn't leave him. In spite of all the money, fame, and beautiful women he fooled around with, he knew Toni was the best thing that ever happened to him. And even though he couldn't remain faithful to her, he loved her just the same and didn't want to let her go.

The thought of her being with another man was out of the question—Toni was his and only his, and he wasn't about to let her go. He knew it was unfair for him to continue to be with other women and expect her to stay with him, but he was a famous rapper now, he didn't have to be fair anymore.

Calvin took the fresh linen, gave Toni a quick slap across her bare ass, and slipped into the bathroom to take his shower.

A couple of hours later, Toni dropped Calvin off at the airport.

"I'll call you as soon as I get to Detroit."

Toni knew better than to wait for a phone call from her husband. She knew that as soon as he got on the airplane, he would forget he even had a wife, much less worry about calling her when he reached his destiny.

"Okay." She smiled and kissed him goodbye. "I love you."

"I love you too, babe." He picked up his carry-on bag and walked away.

She watched as he disappeared into the crowd. As soon as he vanished from sight, her mind quickly went to work. She had to hurry back home to get the semen stashed away under the bathroom sink. She knew that she only had a small window of opportunity to carry out her plan if she wanted to make it work. Smiling to herself, she turned on her heel, hurried out of the airport, and slipped into the front seat of her Jaguar. It was time to go to work.

Chapter Four

Hours later, when Calvin's plane touched down in Detroit, a limousine was waiting at the airport to pick him up and take him to the Anderson Coliseum. Although he wouldn't be performing until the following night, he was scheduled to go by the coliseum to get a tour of the area. Calvin wasn't too thrilled about doing the walk-through however. As he rode in the back of the limo toward the coliseum, he pulled out his cell and quickly dialed Ethan's number to complain. "Yo, E," he said when Ethan answered the phone, "I just got in town. Do I really have to do this shit right now?"

"Yes, they need to show you around tonight so you'll know where everything is tomorrow when you do the show." Ethan wished that Calvin would just do what he was told without complaining, but he knew that wasn't going to happen.

"Why can't they show me around tomorrow when I do the sound check?" He wanted to go straight to his hotel suite, get settled in, and then hit the nightclubs in hopes of getting fucked up and fucked. And here they were, taking him to the coliseum for a walk-through. He didn't have time for this shit. He had to get some of that Detroit pussy.

"Listen, Calvin, stop bitching and do the shit, all right? I'll come by your suite and see how things went as soon as I get there, okay?"

"What time will you make it in?" Calvin lit up a joint and then pulled on it.

"My plane should touch down around ten tonight. I'll be by the suite around eleven or so. You're gonna be in, right?"

"Hell no, nigga." Calvin tried to hold the smoke in. "By eleven I should be neck-deep in pussy." He laughed as he let the smoke out. "Detroit pussy."

"Y'all young brothas, all y'all think about is getting pussy. Now I'm a man and I love the pussy, so don't get it twisted. But y'all young niggas need to realize that there's more to life than pussy."

"Oh yeah—like what?" He took another hit off the joint.

"You need to worry about getting that cheddar. You keep on chasing pussy—mark my words, nigga—that's gonna be your downfall."

"Yeah, well as long as I'm falling down in pussy, then it can be my downfall." He chuckled. Calvin looked out of the window when he felt the limo slowing down. "Yo, man, we here at the coliseum; I'll holla atcha later."

"All right."

Calvin hung up the phone and took another draw off his joint. While holding the smoke in, he quickly put the joint out by squeezing the end with his fingers until the glowing embers disappeared. After slipping the roach in his jacket pocket, he leaned back against the seat, closed his eyes, and slowly blew the smoke out as the mellowing effects of the reefer washed over him. By the time they reached the coliseum, his whole attitude changed due to calming effects of the weed. He chilled while he waited for the driver to open his door.

After completing the walk-through at the Anderson Coliseum, Calvin went back to his suite at the Prescott Plaza Hotel. Considered one of the most prestigious hotels in Detroit, the Prescott often played host to the top hip-hop artists when they came into town. And since Calvin considered himself the best lyricist in the country, he didn't see why he didn't deserve to stay where the best stayed. As he strolled through his spacious suite, he started undressing, all the while taking in the ambience of the room. He was definitely feeling his sleeping quarters for the night.

Along with the standard amenities the hotel provided, such as a Jacuzzi, a double-side, see-through fireplace and fully stocked mini-bar, they also accommodated his own personal requests. The mini-bar was stocked with Hennessy, his drink of choice. Hooked up to the 50-inch Sony plasma TV was his requested PlayStation 2. Sitting next to the PlayStation were his favorite video games—Grand Theft Auto III, Midnight Club 3: Dub Edition, and Madden NFL. The hotel had also provided him with a large fruit basket and a box of imported chocolates.

This is the life, he thought as he tossed his shirt on the king-size bed. Just as he was about to fix himself a drink, there was a knock at the door. He wondered who it could be as he went to answer it.

"Hello," the hotel employee said when Calvin opened the door. She was carrying a gift basket. "This just arrived for you."

"Really," Calvin said as she handed him the basket. He took it and slipped her a few bills. After closing the door, he carried the basket over to the bar and began to examine it. There was a card attached. He removed the card, opened the envelope, and read the note:

I'm proud of you, baby. This is a little something to help you celebrate your success.

> *Love*
> *Your wife, Toni.*

Calvin smiled as he lay the card down. He opened the basket to find a bottle of Cristal. "Alrighty then." He laughed as he grabbed a glass and fixed himself a drink. "Thanks, baby." He took a sip of the champagne. As he nursed on his drink, he kicked off his shoes, compliments of G-Phorce, picked up the remote, and turned on the television. He tossed the remote onto the bed and disappeared into the bathroom to start the shower.

Once he had the water temperature to his liking, he finished his drink, stripped off the rest of his clothes, and stepped into the shower. As he stood under the streaming hot water, he thought about all the trouble he was about to get into tonight. His plans included hitting the clubs, picking up some of the hottest ladies in Detroit and bringing them back to his suite and giving them the fuck of a lifetime.

* * *

Just like Ethan predicted, his plane arrived in Detroit around ten. Unlike Calvin, who had a limousine waiting for him at the airport, Ethan traveled like common folks. He quickly caught a cab over to the Prescott Plaza hotel and checked into his room.

Ethan's room wasn't as plush as Calvin's, but it served its purpose. All he needed was a place to rest his head and he was happy. He didn't require a lot of amenities to be happy, nor did he require a lot of women. In fact the only woman he had designs on was married to the man he was managing.

As he unpacked his bags, he thought about Toni, imagining her curled up in her bed all alone. He imagined what it would be like to be her man, to fly back home to Atlanta, run up the stairs to her bedroom and see her lying there waiting for him. He imagined what it would be like to be in her arms making love to her all night long. As the idea of kissing her, touching her, loving her occupied his thoughts, he felt himself become aroused and smiled at the thought of slipping inside her and filling her womanhood up with his manhood.

But then his mind turned to Calvin. Calvin didn't know how to take care of a woman like Toni; didn't know how to love her the way she deserved to be loved.

"Damn," he mumbled. He shook his head as he thought about how unfair life was. Calvin didn't deserve to be with Toni. She was supposed to be with him. But Calvin was the one who had stolen her heart. He was one lucky-ass nigga and didn't even know it.

As he reached down and adjusted his hard-on, he tried to push Toni out of his mind. He wasn't there to dream about sexing another man's wife; he was there to make sure that Calvin got to where he was supposed to be, when he was supposed to be there, and that was what he was going to focus on.

After he hung up the last few pieces of his wardrobe, he headed upstairs to find Calvin and go over the game plan for the next day. He knocked on Calvin's door and got no answer. He glanced at his watch. It was 11:17. He remembered what Calvin said about being "neck-deep in pussy" by eleven. Knowing Calvin, Ethan was sure that's where he was—probably fucking some sista he barely even knew, while his wife was sitting at home all alone. He shook his head as he pulled out his cell to dial Calvin's number. After three rings, the call went to voicemail.

Yo, man, it's Ethan. I'm in town. Give me a call when you get this." Since he couldn't find his client, he decided to hit one of the local bars for a drink. He'd try to catch up with Calvin later.

Chapter Five

After a few drinks and a couple more unsuccessful phone calls to Calvin, Ethan went back upstairs to see if he could find him in his room. Much to his disappointment, Calvin still didn't answer his door. It was 1:30 A.M. Fed up with his disappearing act, Ethan resigned to catching up with him early the following morning at the radio station.

"Yo, man, where in the hell are you?" he said into his cell phone. "Look, nigga, I'll be by your room first thing in the morning so we can go over your shit, and you better be there." He hung up the phone and shook his head. He was starting to wonder if he was being paid enough to baby-sit this wannabe "bad ass." He slipped the cell in his jacket pocket and headed down the hallway.

When he reached the elevator, there was a young couple along with an older woman waiting for its arrival. He gave them the cursory nod as he pulled out his BlackBerry to check his schedule for the next day: radio interview with KRXW at 10:00 A.M.; radio interview with WSDZ at 11:00

A.M.; Meet & Greet at Circuit City at 12:00; Meet & Greet at Best Buy at 2:00 P.M.; wardrobe fitting at 5:00 P.M.; a quick bite to eat at 6:00 P.M.; sound check at 7:00 P.M.; show starts at 9:00.

When the elevator arrived, Ethan slipped his organizer back into his pocket and waited for the doors to open.

"Oh my God," the younger lady gasped as the doors opened, revealing a semi-naked woman who'd been apparently severely beaten and raped. She lay sprawled out before them on the elevator floor, her bloodied and beaten body motionless as the young man cautiously moved toward her.

"Is she dead?" the girlfriend asked.

"I don't know," the boyfriend mumbled. He kneeled down next to her, placed two fingers at the base of her neck, and waited. "She's alive," he announced, looking back at them.

"Thank God." His girlfriend breathed out a heavy sigh of relief.

"For God sake, cover her up," the older woman said.

Ethan removed his BlackBerry from his pocket and handed the jacket over to the young man. "Here—use this."

"Thanks." The young man spread the jacket over the young woman's bloodied legs.

"Shouldn't we call 911?" The young woman looked over at Ethan.

"I will."

After placing the call to 911, he informed them of their instructions not to move the body because she may have broken bones, and to keep her covered up to try and prevent her from going into shock. As he watched his three new associates busy themselves around the unconscious young lady, he wondered, *What in the hell is this world coming to when a woman couldn't be safe in an elevator in a hotel as prestigious as the one they were standing in?*

Seconds later, hotel security arrived. As the crowd around the elevator grew larger while they waited on the ambulance to arrive, Ethan wondered whether he should hang around to make sure that everything went okay with the young woman or head down to his room. He didn't want to seem insensitive by not staying, but it was getting late and he and Calvin had one hell of a schedule ahead of them. He glanced at his watch. It was already 1:00 A.M., and Calvin hadn't come back to his room yet. Ethan hoped that he wasn't partying too hard. He sure as hell didn't want to drag that young boy all over town if he was hung over. Feeling obligated to ride this incident out, Ethan decided to hang around until the ambulance arrived.

Minutes later, the police and emergency workers arrived at the scene. While the emergency workers gathered the unconscious victim, the police questioned Ethan and the other witnesses.

"I saw what the other people saw," Ethan informed the officer for the third time. "I was waiting for the elevator just like everybody else. When the doors opened, we saw her lying there. She appeared to be unconscious. I gave them my jacket to cover her up and called 911. I didn't hear anything, and I didn't see anything before that."

After giving the officer his contact information and being informed that they were keeping his jacket for evidence, they finally allowed Ethan to leave. As he took the other elevator—they were still collecting evidence from the first one—he glanced at his watch again. It was now 3:00 A.M., and there was still no sign of Calvin. *He's probably deep in some Detroit pussy,* he thought, shaking his head.

Chapter Six

The following morning, the shrill of the alarm clock pierced Ethan's ears, forcing him out of his sleep. He immediately rolled over and turned the alarm off. He glanced at the large glowing numbers on the clock. It was 6:00 A.M. "Ah shit." He rolled back over in the bed on his back. He just got in bed. As he stared up at the ceiling, debating whether to climb out of bed or to steal a few more minutes of shut-eye, the events of the night before slipped into his mind. He remembered waiting for the elevator and then seeing a badly beaten young lady sprawled out on the floor before him. *Was it a dream?* But when the memories came flooding back, he realized that it wasn't—someone attacked a young girl in the hotel elevator and left her there. He wondered how she was doing. Maybe he could call the hospital and check on her, but he didn't have her name.

He finally managed to pull himself out of bed. Then he remembered Calvin. "Damn." He was exhausted, and now he had to find Calvin and make sure he made all his engagements. He was hoping he didn't have to traipse all over town looking for him. As he reached over and picked up his BlackBerry, his mind went into automatic mode. After checking his schedule, he slipped out of bed and headed for the shower.

Minutes later, he emerged with a towel tied around his waist. *Now it was time to get Calvin up and running*. He picked up the phone and dialed his cell.

"Yo, nigga, what's up?" was the greeting Ethan got when Calvin answered the phone.

Relieved to catch up with him, Ethan pushed his hand through his hair and started pacing. "Where in the hell have you been? I was looking for you all night. You know we were supposed to get together last night."

"Yo, man, I was fucked up last night. I got into my room, had a couple of drinks, and then I was out."

"Man, I came by your room several times last night, and I called your room, your cell. Where the hell were you?"

"I was in my room. I told you I stayed in all night."

"Nigga, please . . . you said you were gonna be out chasing booty."

"That was the plan, but when I got to my room, I got real tired. I guess a nigga ain't used to all the flying and shit."

"You're telling me you were in all night?"

"Hell yeah, nigga—what, you can't hear?"

"I hear just fine, Calvin." Ethan exhaled in frustration.

"Good—now stop bitching; you sound like my wife."

"Look, its 6:45 now. The limo will be here at nine to pick us up. I can meet you downstairs and we can grab some breakfast before the car comes."

"All right, man, I'll meet you downstairs at 7:30."

"Cool." After hanging up the phone, Ethan turned on the TV and flipped through a couple of channels before stopping to hear the local news. Maybe he could see what kind of weather they were expecting today.

He disappeared into the bathroom and began to shave as he listened for the weather forecast. But it wasn't the weather forecast that drew him out of the bathroom and back in front of the TV. He sat down on the edge of his bed and stared at the screen as he listened to the reporter.

"Earlier this morning, nineteen-year-old Tamela Waters was found beaten and possibly sexually assaulted in one of the elevators of the Prescott Plaza hotel. Witnesses say that they found the girl unconscious and half-naked in the elevator. She was rushed to St. Francis Medical Center. Doctors say that she has regained consciousness, but police have not been able to question her yet. At this time, they do not have any suspects. However, they are very interested in talking to a young man that witnesses saw her with earlier that evening."

"Tamela," Ethan said when the reporter moved on to other news. *Well, at least she was conscious.* He hoped they would find the guy who did this to her. He stood up and returned to the bathroom to finish shaving.

Meanwhile, across town at St. Francis Medical Center, Dr. Settle accompanied Detectives Crowder and Vinson down the hospital's corridor.

"So she was raped?" Detective Vinson asked the doctor.

"Well, there were signs of penetration, a few tears, some

bleeding, and vaginal swelling. We also collected some bodily fluids that we believe to be semen. The lab is running tests, but I'm almost positive the sex wasn't consensual."

"Do you think she's up for questioning?" Detective Crowder asked.

"She should be, but you'll have to go easy on her; I don't want her to be overtaxed—she's been through hell."

"We understand," Crowder said, "and we won't take up too much of her time; we just need to talk to her while the details of the attack are still fresh in her mind."

"Okay. Let me go in first," Dr. Settle said as they stopped outside of Tamela's door. "I'll let her know that you want to question her and see how she feels about it . . . if she's up to it."

"Just make sure she knows that the sooner we get her statement, the sooner we can get out there and catch this guy," Crowder said.

"I will," she said before slipping into Tamela's room and leaving the detectives waiting outside the door.

As Dr. Settle smiled when she entered Tamela Waters' room and saw her sitting up, a good sign that she was feeling better.

Tamela's boyfriend, Sean Denton, sat by her side and held her hand. Her swollen face was covered with cuts and bruises from the beating she took.

Dr. Settle approached Tamela's bed. "How are we feeling?"

Tamela winced as she looked up at her. Her entire face ached. "I'm okay," she managed through her swollen, busted lips.

Sean stared helplessly down at his girlfriend and gently squeezed her hand.

"Detectives Vinson and Crowder are outside. Do you feel up to answering some of their questions?"

"Yeah." She nodded slightly.

"Are you sure?" Sean asked. She'd only regained consciousness a few hours ago, and he didn't want some detective upsetting her.

She turned her eyes to Sean. "I have to," she whispered, ". . . I have to get him."

Sean nodded and gently squeezed her hand again. He wanted to get this son of a bitch who did this to her.

"Okay," Dr. Settle said, "I'll tell them to be quick." Seconds after Dr. Settle left the room, there was a light knock on the door.

"Come in," Sean called out.

Detectives Daniel Vinson and Amanda Crowder entered the room. "Hello, Miss Waters," she said, "I'm Detective Crowder, and this is my partner, Detective Vinson." She moved to the side of Tamela's bed to shake her hand.

"Hello," Tamela managed.

"I'm her boyfriend, Sean Denton." Sean stood up and shook the detectives' hands.

"Sorry we have to meet under these circumstances." Detective Vinson pulled out his notepad.

"Me too," Sean replied and sat back down.

"Well, Miss Waters, we are going to try to make this as quick as possible. Some of these questions may seem intrusive and embarrassing, but we have to ask them, okay?" Detective Crowder informed her.

Tamela nodded.

"I'm going to ask you to tell me what happened last night when you were attacked, and I need you to be as detailed as possible. Don't leave anything out. The more information you can give us about the attack, the better chance we have of finding out who this guy is and apprehending him."

Tamela looked over at Sean and then at the detectives. "I know who he is," she whispered.

Sean sat up and stared down at her. "You do?" He had just assumed that it was a stranger and had never thought of asking her if she knew the guy.

"You know who your attacker was?" Detective Crowder asked. She gave her partner a quick glance and then looked back at Tamela. "Who?"

Tamela hesitated for a few seconds as she tried to summon the courage to say his name. She closed her eyes as the tears welled up inside her.

"Take your time," Detective Crowder tried to coax Tamela as she stood over her like a cheetah stalking its prey.

Tamela slowly opened her eyes as her heart began to beat faster. "It was that rapper," she said in a low, almost timid voice.

"Rapper?" Sean said. "Which rapper?"

Tamela looked over at him. "Blayze."

"Blayze?" Detective Crowder looked puzzled.

Tamela looked up at her. "His real name is Calvin Wallace. I met him last night at the hotel." She looked over at Sean. "I'm sorry." She began to cry. "I'm so sorry. I just wanted an autograph, and he told me to follow him to his room." She looked back at the detectives. "I got on the elevator with him, and he started coming on to me, trying to kiss me and grabbing at me. I said no. I tried to stop him but I couldn't. He started hitting me. He kept hitting me and trying to pull my clothes off. I started screaming and he kept on hitting

48

me. I don't know what else happened. When I woke up, I was here in the hospital," she sobbed.

Sean leaned forward and tried to gather her in his arms as he fought back his impending tears.

"I'm sorry," she sobbed against his chest. "I'm so sorry."

"It's okay, baby." Sean stroked her hair. "It's okay." He held her trembling body tight.

Detective Crowder turned and looked at Detective Vinson. Vinson tried to remain unaffected by the news. Crowder started toward the door. "Let's give them a minute."

Vinson nodded.

"I'm going to talk with my partner for a minute," she informed Sean as he continued to try to console his girlfriend.

The detectives stepped outside the room. "What do you think?" Crowder asked.

"A rapper sexually assaulting a girl in a hotel elevator sounds a little off-center."

"You think she's lying?"

"No, I don't think she's lying, but it's just a little odd, that's all. Why would he attack her in the elevator and risk getting caught? Why not wait until he gets her back to his room? She was going up to his room with him. That's a huge risk to take, especially if you are a high-profile celebrity."

"So you think she's only telling part of the truth?"

"Maybe. Maybe she's hiding something because her boyfriend's here."

"You suspect the boyfriend?" Crowder asked.

"I don't know, but her story seems a little strange; she seems to be hiding something."

"Well, you saw her. Somebody beat the hell out of her and somebody raped her—that much we know is true. Why would he rape in a public elevator? Who knows why? I don't understand half the shit these rappers rap about, and I sure as hell don't understand why they do what they do."

"Well, we have a victim and now we have a possible suspect. All we have to do is pick him up and see what he has to say, get a sample of his DNA and check it against the DNA from the rape kit."

"This is gonna be a slam dunk. Either he did it, or he didn't; either it matches, or it doesn't."

"And what if it doesn't match?" Vinson asked.

"I've got a feeling it's gonna match."

"Well, if it does match, my son's going to be very disappointed. He listens to that rap crap, and right now the flavor of the month is the kid, Blayze."

"So you've heard of this character?"

"Not only have I heard of him, I've had his music blasting through my house for the past three months now, compliments of Ricky," Vinson said. "And I tell you what—I can't understand a damn thing that guy is saying."

She laughed. "Well, maybe when we pick this guy up, you can ask him to translate for you."

"It may be funny to you, but I've got a sixteen-year-old at home who idolizes this guy."

"Then maybe you can get an autographed picture from this guy too."

"Yeah, yeah," he said. "Now let's get back in there and get the rest of her statement and hopefully pick this guy up tonight."

Chapter Seven

"Hey, man, you look like hell," Calvin said just before he stuffed a forkful of scrambled eggs in his mouth.

"Well, you look like you slept like a baby." Ethan sipped his orange juice. *These young rappers got no upbringing.*

"I did sleep like a baby last night, but tonight I'm hitting the streets." He laughed. "Look out, ladies."

"Well, I was up all night trying to chase you down. And then there was that girl that got raped last night."

Calvin stopped eating and looked up at Ethan. "What girl?" he managed through a mouthful of food.

"You didn't hear? A girl was raped last night right here in this hotel."

"No shit!—in this hotel?"

"Yep. Me and a couple more people found her in the elevator last night. As a matter of fact, I was just leaving your room when we found her on your floor."

"You bullshitting me, man." Calvin laughed and went back to eating.

"Wish I was. Someone had beaten the hell out of that girl, raped her, and left her in the elevator."

"In this fancy-ass hotel?"

"It was on the news this morning. Girl's name is Tamela Waters, I think. Nineteen years old."

"A sista?"

"Yep."

"I guess that means that Kobe's safe." Calvin laughed.

"You're one sick muthafucka."

"Yeah, yeah, yeah. And this sick muthafucka keeps your pockets laced, don't he?"

"True, true. And since I'm being paid me so well, I better get on the job." Ethan glanced at his watch. "The car should be here any minute." He reached into his pocket, pulled a few bills, and tossed it on the table.

Minutes later, they slipped into the back of the limousine. Calvin pulled out a joint.

"Come on, man. Do you have to do that?"

"Yeah, muthafucka—I got glaucoma." He laughed and lit up. He took a hit and then offered Ethan some. "How's your sight, nigga?"

"No thanks, man. I see just fine." He waved the smoke away. "And you don't need to be smoking that shit. You can't walk up into the radio station stinking like pot."

"Nigga, I'm superman. I do what the hell I wanna do. And if those muthafuckas at the radio station have a problem with me getting high, then they can just kiss my pretty black ass." Calvin laughed just before taking another hit off the joint. "A nigga's gotta get crunked up to answer all these dumb-ass questions."

Ethan shook his head and turned his attention to the

streets of downtown Detroit. He wondered how long it would take Calvin to fuck up his career by trying to portray himself as a bad ass.

Rappers couldn't be soft. At least that's what they'd convinced themselves. In order to be respected as a true lyricist, you had to be a bad-ass, above-the-law, shit-talking son of a bitch. And from the looks of it, Calvin was well on his way to being the reigning king of the bad asses. Then he thought about Toni. He wondered what in the hell did she see in this guy and why in the hell did she stick around so long after knowing the way he treated her.

"Yo, man, you all somber and shit. Here we are in Detroit fixing to do our first radio interview and our first major show. Why you looking so perplexed and shit?" Calvin chuckled as he took another hit off the joint.

"I was just thinking," he said as he watched his client getting high.

"Damn, that's the thing about all you college boys—always thinking and shit. Where you go?—Princeton?"

"Yeah." He nodded.

"Graduated top of your class, huh?"

"Something like that."

"And where it get you? All that knowledge they shove in your dome and you sitting here always thinking and shit, worrying and shit. See, a nigga like me don't have to think about shit. Just show up and do my thing."

"You right—us college boys always got something on our minds."

"So what the hell you thinking about, nigga?"

"I was just thinking, here you are, a twenty-four-year-old superstar, making money hand over fist, got women throwing bras and panties and pussy at you in every single direction—why in the hell did you ever marry Toni?"

"That's easy, nigga—I love Toni. I love the hell outta that girl. She's been by my side before people knew who the hell I was; she believed in me when nobody else believed in me; and she's the only woman alive that I trust—that's why I married her."

"Then why in the hell do you run around on her so much and treat her like shit?"

"Because she lets me." Calvin smiled as he finished off the joint and tossed the roach into the ashtray.

Ethan raised his eyebrow as he watched Calvin sit back and get comfortable in his seat. "Because she lets you?"

"Well, it's a little more complicated than that. To understand me and Toni's relationship, you gotta understand our history together. When we started seeing each other, I was a virgin—we both were."

"At seventeen, you were still a virgin?"

"Hey, I was shy, and so was Toni. She was fifteen. We hooked up, started seeing each other, fell in love and shit . . . you know how it goes."

Ethan nodded in agreement.

"I always wanted to be a rapper and shit, but I never told anyone. I didn't think I had the skills, you know. But I knew I could write. I wrote a lot of poetry and shit and I let Toni read them. She was the only person I let read them, me being shy and all. Anyway, she encouraged me to do this rapping shit, to go for it. My girl believed in me. Well, I took a chance. Started working to earn a little change to put together a demo. Then I started humping the streets, trying to get that deal. Finally got close enough to Iceman and slipped him my demo. Shortly after that, Southern Scope Records offered me a deal. That's when shit started happening, man. Started going to all the phat-ass parties, hanging with these phat cats and beautiful ho's. Man, the bitches were so damn fine—phat asses, big-ass tits, tiny-ass waists— and they looking at me and smiling, trying to get with me, a brotha like me that was scared as hell to step to ho's like them."

"But damn, man, you had Toni. Don't take this the wrong way, but your wife is beautiful. She's got all those things that those other women have—except she's the real thing. There's nothing fake about Toni. What in the hell do you need with ho's when you got a lady at home?"

"Nigga, you peeping at my wife?"

"No, man. But how can you not see? How can anybody with eyes not see how beautiful she is, both physically and spiritually?"

"Look, I know Toni's the shit. Hell, I married her, didn't I? But you looking at a nigga who had only been in one pussy all his life. I'd never experienced other women. And then here come these fine-ass bitches, ready to give it up to me just because I know how to flow. Man, I couldn't say no to that. Then once I started kicking it with these other chicks, I just wanted more and more. Toni doesn't like it, but she's learned to live with it. I make the money, she spends the money, and I get to fuck whoever I want to fuck—that's the way it's been for the past few years."

"And you think that's fair to Toni?"

"She'll live."

"And you're the only man Toni's ever been with?"

"Hell yeah, nigga—I better be."

"And what if one day she decided that she wanted to experience other men? How would that make you feel?"

"Not gonna happen."

"But—"

"Not gonna happen."

"You—"

"Listen, nigga, Toni ain't going nowhere, and I definitely ain't sharing with some other nigga. So, as you see, it's not going to happen. End of discussion." He pulled out another joint, lit it up, and took a hit. All this talk about Toni being with another man was bringing down his high fast.

When they arrived at the first radio station, there was a small mob of fans anxiously waiting to get a glimpse of their newest idol. At the sight of his limousine, the crowd went crazy, screaming his name and frantically jumping up and down. Luckily for Calvin, the radio station hired security when they noticed the unexpected mob forming outside their studio earlier that morning in hopes of seeing Blayze.

Calvin marveled at his following. "This shit feels good as hell." He looked over at Ethan and laughed. "These muthafuckas love me."

"Yeah, they love you—let's just hope they don't trample us." *Thank God that the radio station had the foresight to hire security.* It had never crossed his mind. He knew Calvin was blowing up, but he never predicted that his appearance would draw such a crowd. He was still considered a baby in the industry, but it was apparent that he was kicking ass and taking names.

The driver climbed out and opened the door for them. Calvin and Ethan slipped out of the car. The fans screamed frantically, fueling Calvin's already huge ego. Calvin waved to his newfound peeps as security struggled to hold back the mob.

"Blayze, I love you!" one fan yelled. Others screamed, waved his pictures, CD's, and homemade signs.

"I love you too!" he yelled back as security rushed him into the radio station.

As Ethan and Calvin followed the blonde receptionist at the station down the hall to the DJ booth where the interview would be conducted, Calvin studied the way her ass swayed in front of him. He was never into white girls, but this chick had an ass on her that would make a brotha consider flipping the script and getting down with the "white meat." The way her fat, round ass bounced in front of him made him wonder if she had any black in her, and if not, would she like to? He chuckled to himself as he pictured her face down and ass up in his hotel room while he fucked her from behind. The thought of her ass bouncing off of him made his dick hard.

He quickly adjusted himself and he pushed the idea of fucking her out of his mind. He decided to let the white boys keep her. Although she had a banging sista-girl ass and pussy was pussy, he wouldn't dishonor his ebony sistas by letting a white chick bounce up and down on his dick.

Seconds later, the receptionist led him into the DJ booth where DJ Double-D was waiting for him. The DJ immediately rose to his feet and extended his hand to Calvin when they walked into the room.

"Damn, man, it's a pleasure meeting you." He shook Calvin's hand then Ethan's. "I must admit that I'm a huge fan."

"Thanks, man," Calvin responded. "It's always nice to meet a fan."

After the introductions, the DJ informed Calvin about the interview procedures, giving him the heads-up on what he could and could not say on the air. "We're broadcasting live, so you're gonna have to edit yourself, you know . . . because of FCC rules and regulations."

"Cool."

The producer gave Calvin his headphones and instructed him on where to sit. Calvin slipped on the headphones and made himself comfortable in the DJ booth, and Ethan took a seat in the waiting room and began to go over his schedule.

Before starting the interview, the DJ played Calvin's latest number one single, "Priceless," from his number one CD of the same name.

After working on your CD
For so damn long
First time hearing
Radio play your song
Priceless

A trip to Jacob's
To cop me some ice
Sneaks, jeans, throwback
To make a nigga look nice
Fly performance gear
Twelve hundred dollars

Tour bus, rental cars,
30,000 miles to go

Hotel bills, gas, and meals
Giving fans a show
Thirty-city tour
Seventy-five thousand dollars

First time stepping
Onto the stage
Hearing thousands of fans
Screaming your name
Priceless

As the last few beats of the song faded, the DJ turned the mikes back on.

"Okay, we're back," DJ Double D announced into the mike. "And, as promised, we've got the man in the house." He looked over at Calvin. "He's the newest addition to the long list of rappers coming out of the ATL. You know him, you love him, and you've been waiting to see him. Performing live tonight at the Anderson Coliseum here in downtown Detroit, here's Blayze." He pushed the sound effect button, causing the sound of applause to fill the studio.

"Blayze, it's good to have you with us today." He fidgeted with a few controls. "Glad you could stop by."

"Glad to be here."

"For those of you who wanted to see Blayze tonight at the Anderson Coliseum, I'm sorry to say that—but Blayze is probably not—the show's been sold out." He looked over at Calvin. "So, tonight will be your first live performance?"

"Actually, no. I've done a few small shows at local clubs in Atlanta, but this will be my first big show and I'm excited as hell, man."

"I bet you are. Anything the fans should be expecting during the show?"

"They should be expecting the hottest show they've ever seen. Da Backup Brothas will be the opening act, and they are hot as hell too."

"We just played 'Priceless' for your fans. I understand you got the concept from the MasterCard commercial. But why were you inspired to write a song based on the commercial?"

"Well, when we think about entertainers, we don't normally think about all the preparation and money it takes to get that artist's work out to the fans. And even though it costs a great deal to get a CD produced and to deliver live shows like the one tonight, there are moments in an artist's life that are priceless. Like hearing your song on the radio for the first time or stepping out on the stage and knowing that the screams are for you. You can't put a price tag on shit like that." Calvin chuckled.

"Yo, man, watch the language," Double D warned.

"My bad, my bad."

"Cool, cool," the DJ nodded. "Now *Priceless*, the CD has been number one for weeks now. How does it feel having the number one CD in the country?"

"It feels good as hell, man."

"I understand that the CD has been certified triple platinum in three months. How do you account for the success of your sales?"

"I have been very lucky to work with some outstanding producers like Iceman and Fat Boy. They are a dynamic team and help me put together a banging CD. Once the people got a taste of the flavor on the CD, it was bound to take off. I must admit that even though I knew the CD was going to take off, I was surprised it took off so fast."

"Well, you've obviously done your thing on this CD. I got my own copy and I loved it."

"Thanks, I appreciate that, man; I poured my heart and soul into that CD."

"And it shows. Now, as you know, for the past five years, Dollar Bill has been knocking MC's down and guarding the number one spot. Then here you come and, in three months, you have stolen his place on the charts. How does that make you feel?"

"Feels good as hell, man. For years, I have admired Dollar Bill, wishing I could be just like him, wishing he would take me under his wing and show me the ropes, help me get my foot in the door."

"Now you have not only gotten your foot in the door, you have made your presence known. You have stood up and said look at me, respect me, and give me my props. Do you feel like you are competing against Dollar Bill or is there room enough at the top for the both of you."

"Naw, man, Dollar Bill's not my competition. There ain't enough room at the top for both of us; there's only room at the top for one—and that's me. Dollar Bill had his run at the number one spot. Now it's time for him to step down. And if he's not ready to step down then he'll get knocked down."

"Speaking of Dollar Bill, he was a guest on our show about a week ago. We asked him what he thought about you. He said you were a short-timer and wouldn't last long in the music business. He talked about your songs having mad beats but weak lyrics. He also said that you just got lucky and it won't be long before your fans find out you're a fake wannabe rapper. What is your response to his comments?"

"Fuck Dollar Bill and his crew. Dollar Bill is a punk-ass son of a bitch that—"

"Cut, cut!" the DJ yelled to the producer, signaling to him to end the broadcast. He ripped off his headphones, stood up, and stared down at Calvin in disbelief.

The producer quickly interrupted the broadcast. "And now a word from our sponsors."

Calvin pulled off his headphones and stood up.

"Yo, man, watch the language. We're broadcasting this interview live," the DJ said to Calvin. "What . . . you trying to get me fired and shit?"

"Look, muthafucka, this is me. The people love me. You saw that crowd downstairs. They didn't come to see no punk-ass nigga; they came to see Blayze."

"Listen, this is a radio station. We—"

"Fuck the radio station. Y'all can't censor my shit; I'm the hottest muthafucka around here. Damn, I'm the hottest thing in this country and every other country."

Seeing and hearing the argument between Calvin and the DJ unfold right there in front of him, Ethan quickly rose to his feet. He hurried to the DJ booth and attempted to get Calvin's attention and calm him down, but it was too late. The next thing he saw was Calvin punching the DJ, knocking him into the equipment and onto the floor.

"Holy shit!" Ethan raced into the booth and grabbed Calvin. A few more employees rushed in behind him, assisting him in stopping the assault.

Ethan pushed Calvin up against the wall. "What the fuck is wrong with you? Nigga, are you crazy?"

"Fuck that bitch!" Calvin shoved Ethan off and stormed out of the room.

Ethan turned around to help the DJ, but his co-workers had already helped him to feet.

"Yo, man, I'm sorry." Ethan reached into his jacket and pulled out a business card. "We'll take care of this; just give me a call." He thrust the card into the dazed DJ's hand and then rushed out the studio to find Calvin before he did anymore damage.

When Ethan climbed into the limousine looking for Calvin, he found him in the back smoking on another joint. Without saying a word, Ethan sat down across from him.

Calvin took a hit off the joint and watched Ethan, awaiting his reaction or an argument, but Ethan didn't give him one.

Ethan lowered the partition between him and the driver and leaned forward to talk to him. "We're going to WBBX, the radio station."

"Yes, sir."

Ethan sat back in his seat and raised the partition again.

Calvin continued to wait for Ethan's tongue-lashing but didn't get one.

Ethan busied himself with his BlackBerry, checking the schedule, and placed a few phone calls.

After realizing that Ethan didn't intend to chew him out, Calvin lay his head back and closed his eyes, enjoying the effects of the pot.

When the limo pulled up to the next radio station, thirty minutes earlier than scheduled, Calvin could take no more of the silent treatment. "Aren't you going to say anything?" He tossed the roach into the ashtray and stared at Ethan.

"What am I supposed to say?"

"I guess you were supposed to scold me or some shit like that, ask me what the hell is wrong with me jumping on the DJ like that."

"Well, I don't have to ask you what's wrong with you 'cause you and I both know that you're crazy as hell. And as far as scolding you . . . you are a grown-ass man; I don't have to scold you. You know right from wrong. There is nothing I can do to get you to act with some decorum. It's up to you to get your shit together. I'm just going to continue to baby-sit you like I'm paid to do and hope like hell you don't kill yourself or anyone else. And if you hurt anyone like you did that DJ in there, they will take care of you—you're making the money now. They are just waiting for you to jump on them, hoping you'll hit them, so they can turn around and sue your pretty black ass, take all your hard-earned money and put you back on the streets where you started—broke and busted. But they won't, because your bad-ass reputation will be too much of a liability. So with all that going for you, I don't need to say shit—it's your livelihood on the line. I can find another rapper to baby-sit. There are about a hundred thousand other wannabe rappers waiting to take your place just like you took Dollar Bill's, so it won't be hard for me to replace you."

Calvin stared at Ethan. He was baffled by his calm and un-ruffled disposition. He displayed no signs of stress or anger by the fight earlier. Calvin was put off by this and didn't know how to respond. "Well, let's do this," he finally as he climbed out of the limousine.

"Let's," Ethan replied, following him.

Chapter Eight

A few hours later, at the Anderson Coliseum, Da Backup Brothas, the opening act for Blayze, finished their last song and raced off the stage, leaving the crowd in a screaming frenzy. The massive coliseum held 15,000 seats, and from the screams that filled the arena, it was obvious that every ticket holder was present and accounted for.

Before the MC could take his place on the stage, the crowd began to chant, "Blayze, Blayze, Blayze, Blayze," as they waited for him to make his appearance. Their enthusiasm fueled Calvin's already enormous ego.

"This is what I'm talking 'bout," Calvin said to Ethan as he waited for his cue backstage. "You hear that shit?—that's for me . . . all that shit." Calvin laughed.

Though he wouldn't admit it, he was nervous. This was the first time he would be performing for such a large crowd. That, along with the enormous record sales, added a lot of pressure. He had to do his thing, give the people what they wanted. He had to kick ass. He couldn't disappoint the thousands of fans supporting him. He swallowed hard.

Ethan could read the anxiety on his face. Though Calvin still tried to sound cocky and confident, Ethan saw a glimmer of hope that this smart-ass, wisecracking, take-no-prisoners rapper did have feelings beyond telling someone off or kicking someone's ass. Calvin was actually nervous. This was the first time since he had been hired to baby-sit the star that he had seen a real human being.

Ethan smiled. *Maybe there's hope for this guy.*

Calvin wrung his hands as he paced the floor. "This is for my peeps," he mumbled to himself.

Ethan stepped in his path. He grabbed Calvin by the shoulders and stopped him. "Yo, man, you got this—you know this and I know this. Hell, the whole world knows this. That's why you've sold over three million copies of your CD. That's why this and three more of your concerts are already sold out. That's why they are out there screaming your name. This is your thing, man; this is what you do."

Calvin looked at his manager with newfound confidence. "You're right, nigga." He laughed. "This is what I do."

"C'mon, everybody, make some noise if you're having a good time," the MC said.

The crowd roared.

"All right, people, who did you come to see?"

"Blayze!"

"Who?"

"Blayze!"

"Are you sure you want to see him?"

"Yeah!"

"He's sold over three million copies of his debut CD, *Priceless*, has the number one single in the country, and is hot like fire. Please, put your hands together and welcome to the stage Southern Scope recording artist and the newest rhyme master hailing from Atlanta, Georgia—the bad boy himself, Blayze."

"That's you." Ethan smiled and slapped him on the back.

"Hell yeah, that's me. Watch me do my thing, nigga." He took a deep breath and then raced onto the stage.

The crowd roared.

"What up, Detroit? Let me hear you make some noise!" He surveyed the mob of screaming fans. "Yeah . . . now that's what I'm talking 'bout—Detroit's in the muthafuckin' house."

The crowd was in a mad frenzy.

Calvin took a few minutes to enjoy the hysterics over him. Then as the crowd began to calm down, he brought the microphone to his lips. "I want to tell y'all something."

The crowd screamed again.

"I just learned yesterday that my CD has been certified triple platinum."

The crowd roared.

He chuckled. "Y'all make a nigga proud, make a nigga wanna get all soft and shit and cry."

More screams.

"Because y'all gave a brotha a chance and went out and got my album, because y'all made my CD number one in the country, I'm gonna drop a little something for you off the top of my head to let you know how I feel."

Waves of screams vibrated through the dark coliseum as colorful overhead lights danced over the ecstatic fans. Calvin looked over at his DJ. He had an earphone on one of his ears, and with his hunched-up shoulder, stood poised over two turntables as he waited for Calvin's signal.

"Yo, Tweak, give me a little something-something." Calvin then turned his attention back to the audience. As Tweak dropped the beat, Calvin strolled around the stage, watching his fans and trying to find the words to express what he was feeling. "Are y'all ready for this?" He bobbed his head to the mad beats his DJ was kicking out.

The coliseum roared, "Yeah."

"Yeah, yeah, yeah, yeah, it goes a little something like this . . ." He walked to the center of the stage.

Two years ago
Had pen, paper and a dream
Nigga trying to cash up
Make a little cream
Never asking for a handout
Just asked for a hand
But niggas mean-mugging
Wouldn't give a nigga a chance

Making sure everybody got a taste, he raced over to left side of the stage and continued flowing.

Armed with my demo
And my will to succeed
Just listen, one listen
That's all a nigga need
And that's all it took
My lyrics hit his ears

Took a brotha under his wing
That's how I got here

Three million sold
More than I ever dreamed of
All because one man
Showed a young nigga love
I've stolen the number one spot
I've just stepped in the game
I'm here muthafuckas
So say my muthafuckin' name

As he bounced to the beat of the music, the hot swirling overhead lights made him sweat. His throwback jersey and baggy jeans clung to his sweat-drenched body, while the ice that dripped from his neck, wrists, and ears sparkled. While grabbing the crotch of his sagging jeans that were obviously too big for him, he raced over to the right side of the stage and yelled into his mike. "Any of you muthafuckas know who the hell Dollar Bill is?"

The massive crowd screamed.

"Any fans of Dollar in the house?"

They screamed again.

"This little part here is for all you Dollar Bill fans." He watched the crowd bounce up and down, cheering him on.

Dollar Bill called me short-timer
Say my lyrics ain't shit
Here's some lyrics for you Dollar Bill
Suck my muthafuckin' dick

Then suck my left nut
And make my right one jealous
Then kiss my pretty black ass
You sorry muthafucka

His fans went ballistic as he continued to flow.

An hour later, Detectives Vinson and Crowder made their way backstage as they followed the Anderson Coliseum security.

"Mr. Wallace is performing at this time, but you can wait back here for him." The security guard showed them where they could wait. "I've got to get out front to help control the crowd."

"Look who's here," Detective Vinson said when he noticed Ethan backstage, working on his BlackBerry. He looked at his partner. "Let's go over and say hello."

"Mr. Michaels."

Ethan looked up from his BlackBerry to see the officers approaching. "Don't tell me you're fans—you should've told me; I would have given you tickets."

"We're not fans; we're here on official police business."

"Oh, you're here about the incident at the radio station?"

"Radio station?" Vinson glanced over at his partner.

"Calvin has a little bit of a temper. He's just trying to be a bad ass, but he's harmless."

"Well, actually, we're not here about the radio station," Crowder informed him. "We're here about the rape at the Prescott Plaza hotel last night."

"The girl in the elevator?"

"Yes."

"So you're here to see me—how is she doing? I heard she regained consciousness."

"She's doing fine. But we're not here to talk to you, we're here to pick up Calvin Wallace for the assault on Miss Waters."

"What? Calvin? You're saying Calvin raped her?"

Vinson nodded. "She identified him as her attacker."

"Not Calvin. It must be some kind of mistake. I know he's a bad ass and all, but he's no rapist."

"Well, that's not what our victim says. And now that we have you here, you can come down to the station with us and answer some questions as well," Crowder told him.

"Your continued cooperation would be greatly appreciated," Vinson added.

"Not a problem," Ethan said, still stunned by the accusation. "I'll help as much as possible, but I'm sure this is some kind of mistake. I know Calvin—he's not capable of doing something like this. Like I said, he's a bad ass, but he's no rapist. He's a married man. He's a rapper, for God sake—he's got women throwing themselves at him all day long; he doesn't have to beat a woman to get sex. Why in the hell would he have to take it when he has so many women ready to give it to him freely?"

"Contrary to popular belief," Crowder said in a sarcastic tone, "not all women want to sleep with a rapper. Maybe our victim is a woman of discriminating taste. Now how much longer does he have?"

"About another hour."

"I don't think I can listen to this noise for another hour," Crowder said.

"Me neither—let's pick him up."

"You can't be serious. You can't pick him up in the middle of his show. He has thousands of fans—"

"Yeah," Vinson interrupted, "and we have a girl in the hospital that was nearly beaten to death because she said no. So forgive me if we are anxious to take in your client."

With that, the detectives walked onto the stage toward Calvin. "Mr. Wallace," Detective Vinson called out as they approached him during the middle of his performance.

He stopped rapping and looked over at them. "What in the hell—"

The officers pulled out their badges and showed it to him. Thinking it was part of the show, the crowd roared even louder.

"What in the hell is going on?" he asked once the detectives were within earshot.

As he pulled out his handcuffs, Vinson began to Mirandize him. "You have the right to remain silent."

"You can't be fuckin' serious," Calvin said when he saw the cuffs. "This is some kind of joke, right? Am I getting punked?"

Vinson grabbed one of his wrists and placed the cuffs on it. "If you give up the right to remain silent"—He cuffed the other wrist—"anything you say, can and will be used against you."

"Yo, Ethan, man, this is a fuckin' joke, right?"

"Look, Calvin, I'm going to call your lawyer. Don't say a word," Ethan warned him. He knew Calvin wasn't going to go without putting up a fight.

"My lawyer?—what do I need my lawyer for? This is a joke, right?" He was becoming agitated; they were taking the joke too far.

"It's not a joke, Calvin."

"Mr. Wallace, you're under arrest for the sexual assault to Tamela Waters," Detective Crowder finally informed him.

"What? Oh hell, no! This has gone too far. Let me go."

Realizing that something was wrong, the crowd's cheers began to turn to boos.

Once his hands were secure behind his back, Vinson began patting him down. "You don't have any knives, needles or sharp objects in your pockets, do you?"

"No," he said looking around. "Where's Ashton? Ashton, you get your punk ass out here!" he yelled.

"Do you have any guns, drugs, on you that we should know about?" Vinson continued to pat him down.

"No, muthafucka; now let me go." Calvin began to struggle.

"Calvin, don't resist." Ethan tried to warn him. "We'll get this sorted out."

"Hell no, muthafucka!" He tried to pull away from the detective.

"You're only making it worse for yourself, Mr. Wallace." Crowder reached for her pepper spray.

By that time, Detective Vinson and Calvin had fallen to the floor as Calvin continued to try to free himself.

The crowd began to lose it. They started throwing bottles, cans, and any other items they could put their hands on. Security fought to hold back the angry mob as they tried to rush the stage and protect their idol.

Realizing that they didn't have much time to get him off-stage before the mob attacked, Crowder grabbed a handful of Calvin's hair, pulled his head back, and sprayed him in the eyes with the pepper spray.

"Oh shit!" Calvin screamed out as the spray burned his

eyes. Then he started coughing and gasping for air. He could feel his throat and chest closing up as his breathing became constricted.

"Calvin, stop fighting!" Ethan yelled.

But Calvin continued to struggle under Vinson's weight. He tried to open his eyes, but the burning was so intense, it was useless. He lost control of his limbs and was no longer able to put up a fight.

When Vinson felt his resistance fade, he stood up and pulled Calvin to his feet with Crowder's assistance. They held him up and hastily dragged his limp body offstage before the mob of fans pounced on them.

Minutes later, they threw him in the back of their car and headed downtown to the station.

Chapter Nine

An hour later, an irate Calvin was retrieved from the holding cell. Although most of the effects of the pepper spray had worn off, his eyes still held a hint of redness and burned slightly. He remained calm as the officer led him down the hall; he didn't want another shot of the pepper spray. The only thing he wanted was to find out what in the hell was going on.

Detective Vinson led him down to the interrogation room while his partner followed. They came to a small room that contained a rectangular metal table and three folding chairs. On one of the walls was a two-way mirror. Calvin glanced over at it, knowing that there was probably an audience behind it.

"Have a seat." Vinson directed him toward one of the chairs.

Calvin sat down without saying a word. He just watched the detectives plan their attack and half-heartedly hoped that he was being punked by Ashton Kutcher.

"Mr. Wallace." Detective Crowder walked over to where

Calvin was, leaned on the table, and looked down at him. "You do understand the charges brought against you, don't you?"

"Hell no," he snarled.

"Well, let me enlighten you—you've been accused of rape—do you understand now?"

"Hell, no," he repeated, "'cause I ain't raped nobody. So you muthafuckas can let me go."

"Sure, we'll let you go as soon as you answer a few questions for us." Detective Vinson strolled over to the two-way mirror and pretended to fix his tie.

"What kind of questions?"

Vinson turned around to face him. "Where were you this morning between 12:30 and 1:00 A.M.?"

"I was in my room sleeping."

"Alone?"

"Hell yeah, alone."

"Is there anyone who can verify that you were in your room asleep at this time?"

"No. I did say that I was alone, didn't I?"

"How convenient." Vinson looked over at his partner.

"Mr. Wallace, you're a rapper, right?" Crowder asked. She pulled out a chair and sat down next to him.

"Well, I was rapping when you two picked me up—if this is the best Detroit has to offer, then I feel sorry for the people here."

"My point is, Mr. Wallace, is that you don't seem the type to be in bed that early. Here you are visiting our fair city. I would think you would be out enjoying yourself, enjoying the nightlife, the beautiful women of Detroit."

"I was tired." He smiled sarcastically.

"Jetlag, huh?"

"I guess. Look, I didn't rape anyone. I got in yesterday, went to the coliseum to take a tour, checked in the hotel around 9:00, took a shower, and went to sleep—that's it. That's all I did. Now I don't know who this chick is, but she's obviously made a mistake. I'm sorry she was hurt, but I ain't the one and you ain't gonna pin this shit on me."

Vinson tossed a few Polaroid pictures of Tamela on the table in front of Calvin. The photos were taken earlier at the hospital to document her injuries from the assault. "Do recognize her?"

Calvin looked at the photos and cringed just before pushing them away. "Damn! Somebody really fucked her up."

"Somebody did; she says it was you."

"Wasn't me." He casually leaned back in his chair and crossed his arms. "I've never seen this chick before."

"Then why is she trying to pin this on you?"

"Hell if I know."

Just then his attorney rushed into the interrogation room. "Mr. Wallace, don't say another word." He pulled out his card and handed it to Crowder. "Joseph Raymond, counsel for the accused," he announced and lay his briefcase on the table. He looked over at Calvin. "Your manager called me and said you needed representation. From this point forward, I advise you not to speak to the police without me being present."

"Yo, man, I don't need an attorney; I didn't do anything."

"Well, your manager obviously thinks you need one. And from what he says, I'm inclined to agree with him." Looking over at Crowder, the lawyer said, "And what has my client been charged with?"

"Aggravated rape." Crowder slid the folder across the table toward him.

Joseph flipped the folder open and read the charges.

"We were just about to inform your client that the victim identified him by name as the man who assaulted her." Vinson looked over at Calvin. "And she was one hundred percent sure that you were her attacker."

"And I'm telling you it wasn't me, so get off my fuckin' back."

"Mr. Wallace—" Joseph tried to caution Calvin.

"Nigga, please . . ." Calvin said as if he was talking to one of his boys. Joseph was appalled by his comment, but Calvin didn't care. Calvin looked over at Crowder. "What do I have to do to prove I didn't touch that girl?—I've got a tour to finish, and I don't have time for this bullshit."

Crowder looked at Vinson and then looked back at Calvin. "Well, since you're being so cooperative, how about giving us a DNA sample?"

"A DNA sample?"

"Mr. Wallace, let me handle this."

"Look, I'm trying to cooperate with these people so I can get the hell out of here."

"But they are just trying to pin this on you. Let's not help them, all right?"

"Help them do what? Help them prove I'm innocent. I didn't do anything. I didn't rape this girl. I have nothing to hide."

"Yes, but I'm asking you not to give these guys anything that they can use against you; I'm trying to save your ass here."

"I didn't ask you to save my ass."

"Isn't that what you are paying me for? Listen, Mr. Wallace, if you are not going to listen to me, then how am I supposed to help you? You need to do what I tell you."

"First of all, I ain't paying you shit. Second of all, all I need to do is stay black and die."

"Listen," Joseph said in frustration, "I can't help you with an attitude like that."

"Then get to stepping, nigga. I don't need a lawyer; I'm innocent."

"I know . . . so just let me help you prove it."

"Nah, you can get to stepping."

"You can't be serious."

"To quote my man, Donald Trump—'You're fired.' Now get the hell outta my face."

His lawyer stared at him in disbelief.

"To be such a highly educated lawyer, you don't seem too bright right now. Maybe if I say it a little slower you'll get it— get-the-hell-outta-my-face."

"That's your ass." Joseph stood up and closed his briefcase. He looked at the detectives. "Sorry to interrupt," he said, and with those words he left.

"Now back to what we were talking about. Tell me about this DNA sample you want."

Crowder told him, "We'll take you to the hospital, get the sample, have a doctor examine you—"

"Have a doctor examine me? For what?"

"Well, the victim was brutally beaten. Her attacker would have injuries to his hands. And if she scratched you, then there would be physical evidence of that as well."

"Well, take a look then." Calvin offered up his hands for them to examine.

Both officers glanced at his hands and didn't see any obvious injuries to them. "The doctors are more capable than we are in assessing your injuries than we are," Crowder informed him. She glanced over at Vinson and then back at Calvin. "Are you willing to go to the hospital and give us a sample?"

"Abso-fuckin'-lutely. If I have to do it to clear my name, I will do it."

Across the hall in interrogation room #3, Ethan was losing his patience with another detective as he tried to answer his questions.

"Listen, I told you, we found the girl in the elevator. She was already unconscious. *We* called the police."

"And you didn't see anyone in the hall prior to finding the girl?" Detective Adams asked.

"The only people I saw prior to finding the girl were the people at the elevator that discovered her with me."

"And you were up on the eighth floor at 1:30 A.M. because . . ."

"I was trying to find Calvin. We were supposed to be meeting to discuss the plans for the next day."

"But you couldn't find him?"

"He was asleep in his room."

"And how do you know that if you couldn't find him?"

"He told me he was asleep the next day."

"But you went to his room and knocked. That didn't wake him up?"

"I guess he's a sound sleeper."

"You guess? You don't know?"

"This was our first time traveling together. I'm not sure if he's a heavy sleeper or not."

"Did you try calling Mr. Wallace? He could have been out partying."

"I called him several times, but he didn't answer."

"So you got in town around 10:30, checked into the hotel around 11:00, and you were strolling the halls of the hotel up to 1:00 A.M. looking for Mr. Wallace. Why were you so anxious to find him?"

"I wanted to make sure we were on the same page for the next day."

"That seems a little extreme, don't you think? Weren't you exhausted just as much as Mr. Wallace claims he was? Didn't you just want to go to bed?"

"I was exhausted, but I'm a perfectionist; I wanted to make sure that things went according to plan."

"Are you sure you weren't looking so hard for Mr. Wallace because you were trying to keep him out of trouble?" Detective Adams flipped through his notes. "From what I gather, you informed Detectives Crowder and Vinson that Mr. Wallace was a bad ass, is that true?"

"Yes but—"

"And is it true that Mr. Wallace has a temper—if he doesn't get what he wants, he blows up?"

"No—"

"But didn't he attack the DJ at the radio station earlier today because he got upset?"

Ethan didn't know what to say. He stared at the officer. *Calvin is in a shitload of trouble.*

* * *

"So what do you think?" Crowder asked Vinson as they waited at St. Francis Medical Center while the doctor examined Calvin.

"I don't know. He seemed awfully anxious to give us a DNA sample and to be examined by the doctor."

"I know. And his hands didn't look like they had any injuries."

"Yeah, something doesn't seem right here."

"Well, we'll have our evidence one way or the other, once we get the lab results back."

A few minutes later, the detectives were baffled over the results of the examination.

"Are you saying that he has no injuries to his hand?" Crowder asked.

Doctor Milton handed them her notes. "Not one."

They looked them over. "But shouldn't there have been some injuries?" Vinson asked. "The way that girl was beaten. How is that possible?"

"The only way he wouldn't have any damage to his hand during that assault was if he used something else or if he wore some thick gloves. And," Milton added, "the injuries were definitely caused by someone's hands."

Crowder speculated. "So he must have worn gloves? It's the middle of summer. He must have known he was going to rape her or somebody else."

"That's if he was the one that raped her." Vinson looked at Crowder.

"You don't think it's him?" Crowder asked.

"Don't know. He doesn't act like someone who's guilty, but we'll know as soon as we get the results from the DNA tests."

Dr. Milton spoke up. "Look, I have to see some more patients. You're more than welcome to use my office."

"Thanks," Vinson said. Then to Crowder, "What do you make of this?"

Before Crowder could answer, her cell rang. "Hello," she said. After finishing her conversation with the caller, she hung up the phone. "That was Johnson and Pruitt with the preliminary results from the room search."

By the look on her face, Vinson knew it wasn't very good news. "What did they find?"

"Nothing really. They went through everything and didn't turn up anything—no blood, no torn clothes, no gloves."

"Maybe he got rid of it, sent it out."

"They questioned housekeeping. Nothing was sent out to be cleaned and when they cleaned the room, they didn't remember seeing any blood."

"He must have gotten rid of the clothing then. There has to be something with her blood on it," Vinson insisted.

"They're sending the clothes to the lab to see what they can find, but it doesn't look good. I have a bad feeling about this. This guy doesn't act like a man guilty of rape; he's too cooperative."

Vinson jogged Crowder's memory. "He did put up a fight at the coliseum."

"He did, didn't he?"

"So when are you'll going to release me?" Calvin asked from the back of the patrol car as they transferred him back to the station.

"You won't go before the judge until Monday, so you'll be

spending a couple of nights as a guest of the state," Crowder informed him.

"You can't be serious. I have to stay locked up all week-end? What about the DNA tests?—that should have cleared me."

"The sample you gave has to be sent off to the lab and that takes a few days to get the results."

"Son of a bitch," he mumbled. Then he thought about Toni. He wondered if Ethan had called her to tell her what was going on. He also didn't get his one call yet. "What about my one phone call? I still get my one phone call, don't I?"

"Yes, you do. You can make it as soon as we get back at sta-tion."

Toni rolled over in her bed as the ringing of the phone awakened her. She glanced at the clock as she picked up the receiver. It was 1:45 A.M. "Hello," she said; her voice thick with sleep.

"Toni, it's Calvin."

"Yeah." She wondered why he was calling at that time of the morning. "What's going on?"

"Babe, I've been arrested."

"Arrested?" She immediately sat up. "For what?"

"Rape. I was arrested for rape."

"Rape. What the hell are you talking about?"

"Some chick said I raped her. But it's okay. I'm just calling you to let you know what's up."

"It's okay?" She climbed out of bed and started anxiously pacing the floor. "What do you mean, 'it's okay'? You've been arrested for rape."

"It's okay, Toni. I didn't rape nobody, you know me." He tried to remain casual so she would calm down.

"But why—"

"It's just a mistake, that's all. I don't know the girl, never met the girl, have never seen the girl. It's just a case of mistaken identity."

"Oh my God," she said, her voice trembling, as she pushed her hand through her hair.

"Calm down, Toni. No need for you to get upset."

"Okay, okay, where are you?" she asked frantically. "I'm coming to get you."

"Look, I'm gonna be locked up until Monday. That's when I get to see the judge so they can set my bail."

"Oh my God."

"I gave them some DNA, and once the lab finishes with it, then they'll realize that this is all a mistake."

"Calvin, why are you so calm? You've been arrested for rape, don't you understand—rape?"

"Because I know I didn't do it, and it's only a matter of time for them to find out that I'm telling the truth."

"I'm coming to see you."

"Baby," he tried to reassure her, "there is no need for that." But it was to no avail.

Chapter Ten

"Hey, Vinson." Crowder walked up to his desk. He looked up from his paperwork. "What's up?"

"We may have a break. I just got a call from the Prescott Plaza hotel. You won't believe our luck."

"What happened?"

"They have surveillance cameras in the elevators."

A smile crossed Vinson's face. "So the attack was caught on tape?"

"Evidently," she smiled. "They want us to come by and take a look at it."

"Well, what are we waiting for?" Vinson picked up his jacket. "Let's check it out."

Thirty minutes later, they arrived at the hotel.

"This can't be good for business," Vinson said as he and Crowder followed John Stapler to his office.

John was the head of security at the hotel and didn't like the negative publicity the hotel was getting from the attack. "No, this is not good for the hotel at all, so the quicker we can help you solve this, the better off we are."

"I understand. So what do we have?" Vinson asked once they were inside the security office.

"Take a look for yourself." Stapler picked the tape up off the edge of his desk and slipped it into the VCR. "Now this is shot from above, so you really can't see the man's face. But this still may help you in identifying him."

Crowder took a seat while Vinson stood behind her with his arms crossed. They waited while Stapler turned on the monitor.

"It's already cued up." Stapler looked back at the detectives and then back at the monitor. When the picture became visible, he stepped out of their way to give them a full view.

Crowder and Vinson both leaned forward to study the scene that played out in front of them.

The elevator doors opened, and a man and woman stepped inside. Their faces were not visible, but the detectives noticed that the woman's clothes matched the victim's.

"That's our victim," Crowder said.

"Yeah, but is that our perp?" Vinson peered at the screen, trying to get a better look at the man.

"Could be. He resembles him from this angle."

The couple appeared to be having a friendly conversation . . . until the man moved closer to the woman. He pulled her into his arms and tried to kiss her, but she rejected his advances, pushing him off.

Crowder looked up at Vinson and then looked back at the screen.

The man tried again to get closer to the woman, and again she rejected his advances. He advanced toward her again, this time with more aggression, shoving her into the corner while his hands groped her.

The woman struggled to free herself, but he was too strong for her. While holding her captive with one arm, he hit the elevator's break button with his free hand. The woman tried to scream, but the man covered her mouth. He tried to rip off her clothes, but he couldn't manage that and keep her quiet.

Finally, after several unsuccessful attempts to undress her, he pulled his hand away from her mouth, stepped back away from her, and started punching her in the head and face.

Crowder winced.

The woman tried to cover her head with her arms and hands to escape his blows, but it was useless. He continued to pummel her with his fist until she fell to the floor. And as if he wasn't satisfied, he dropped down on her and continued to beat her until she lay motionless beneath him.

"My God," Crowder whispered, "this guy is an animal."

Once he realized she was unconscious, he hoisted up her skirt and tore her panties off.

Crowder swallowed as she tried to fight off the wave of sickness that was coming over her.

The man hastily pushed the woman's legs apart and positioned himself on his knees. He quickly undid his pants and pushed it and his underwear down to his thighs. Within seconds, he was on top of her, raping her.

Crowder could take no more. She stood up and walked to the door.

Vinson's eyes remain glued to the monitor as he watched the assault. The victim's face was in clear view. It was Tamela Waters. Then Vinson noticed something about the rapist.

"Stop the tape," he said to Stapler. He moved closer to the monitor to get a better look.

"What is it?" Crowder asked, turning around to watch him.

He motioned her with his hand. "Come here."

Crowder walked over to where he was standing. "What?"

"Look at his right buttock."

Crowder took a closer look.

"What do you think that is?" Vinson asked.

"I don't know—a tattoo . . . maybe a birthmark?"

"I think it's a birthmark. It looks like a birthmark to me."

"It does." Crowder looked at Vinson. "And if Mr. Wallace has that same birthmark on his right buttock, then we have our rapist."

"Yes." Vinson looked away from the monitor and at his partner. "Then Mr. Wallace won't be able to deny it any longer—everything is right here on tape." He looked over at Stapler. "We're gonna need to confiscate that tape as evidence."

"No problem." Stapler pushed the eject button on the VCR. "I'm glad we could help." He handed the tape to Vinson. "Let us know if there is anything else we can do to assist you. We don't need a rapist running around in our hotel, preying on our guests."

Minutes later, Vinson roused Calvin from his sleep. "Wake up, sleeping beauty," he said as he entered his cell.

Still half-asleep, Calvin looked at Vinson as he towered over him. "I'm going home?" He sat up on the edge of his bed.

"Not exactly. Now stand up."

"What the hell do you want?" Calvin was starting to tire of being treated like a common criminal.

"I want you to drop your pants."

"Drop my pants?—nigga, you must be crazy. I know I'm locked down and shit, but damn, I don't go that way. Hell, I thought the prisoners were the only ones fuckin' each other up the ass."

"Don't flatter yourself; I'm just looking for something."

"You're still crazy as hell if you think I'm gonna let you play with my dick." Calvin laughed as he began to climb back into bed.

"Well, you can either drop your pants and possibly get out tonight, or we can wait and I can get a few other officers to pull your pants down for me."

Calvin stood back up and thought about his options. "If I drop my pants and you find or don't find what you're looking for, I could be released tonight?"

"Exactly. I'm looking for evidence that could set you free tonight."

"Then why in the hell didn't you say so in the first place?" Calvin unfastened his jeans. "Hey, where's your partner?— I'd much rather have her look me over." He smiled.

"Just show me your ass."

"Sure, and while you're back there, why don't you bend over and kiss it?" He pushed his pants and underwear down and turned around, revealing his buttocks to the detective. "Pretty ass, huh?"

There it is. Vinson stared at the birthmark on Calvin's right buttock and smiled. "I'll tell you what—you can let some of those cellmates you're going to be living with for the next fifteen-to-twenty years kiss your ass."

Calvin pulled his pants back up and turned to face Vinson. "What do you mean by that? You should be releasing me tonight."

"Actually, Mr. Wallace, I think you're gonna be with us for a while. You see, the hotel has surveillance cameras in their elevators. This means that the rape of Miss Waters was caught on videotape. And guess whose ass was starring in that videotape with Miss Waters?—never mind, I'll tell you—yours."

"What the hell are you talking about? I told you I didn't rape that girl or any girl. That's not me in the video."

"Well, it may not have been you, but your ass made a showstopping debut. So, make your ass comfortable; it's gonna be here for a while."

Chapter Eleven

"We'll talk in the limo," Ethan informed Toni as he carried her bags through the airport. Surrounded by reporters, they hurried as they tried to avoid the mob's questions. Ethan tried to keep the press away from Toni, but they were adamant about getting a statement from her.

One reporter shoved the microphone in Toni's face. "Can you give us a comment about your husband's situation?"

"No comment." Ethan pushed the mike away.

The questions were coming fast and furious. "Have you spoken with your husband since his arrest?" another reporter asked.

"What do you think about the charges of rape? Do you think he's guilty?"

"Are you aware of all the evidence they have against your husband? The victim identified him as her attacker. Do you believe her? Have you spoken with her?"

Ethan wrapped one arm around Toni and maneuvered his way through the crowd. "Don't say a word," he told her.

She clung to him and ignored the questions that the press bombarded her with.

Finally, they made it to their awaiting car. Once settled in the back of the limo, he offered her a drink to calm her nerves.

"No thanks. Just tell me what's going on. How bad is it?"

Before he could answer, Toni's cell phone rang. "Excuse me." She checked the caller ID. It was her mother. "Not again," she mumbled. Toni turned the phone off and put it back in her purse.

"You're not answering it?"

"It's just my mom. It's her fifth call today. She's trying to find out what's happening with Calvin. I told her I didn't know anything and I'll call her back later." Toni reached over and touched Ethan's hand. "Now tell me—what's going on?"

"I'm not going to lie to you. It looks pretty bad. He doesn't have an alibi for the time during the attack. The girl identified him as her attacker, and they have the attack on video."

"Oh my God." Toni brought her hand to her mouth. "Videotape?"

"Yeah, and although they can't see his face on the tape, the attacker and Calvin have the same birthmark in the same location—on their right buttock."

"Oh my God." Toni was on the verge of tears.

"Toni"—Ethan placed his hand on her lap—"he looks guilty."

She stared at him through teary eyes. "No, he didn't do this. Calvin would never do this. You don't believe he's guilty, do you?" She searched his eyes for an answer.

"No," he said quickly, not to upset her. "I don't think he's guilty. There's just so much evidence against him; I think they're going to pin this on him."

"What did his lawyer say?"

Ethan shook his head. "Calvin fired him."

"Oh no! Why?"

"You know Calvin, he's hard-headed and won't listen to anyone."

"Have you seen him?"

"Not since he's been arrested. I've been busy trying to manage the bad press this is getting him. The media is trying to rip him apart."

"I know. I hate this."

"So do I. Now I'm going to take you to see him, but first thing we're going to do is get you settled in at your hotel."

"No, we have to go straight to the jail; I have to see him now. He needs me."

"He can wait, Toni. I want to get you settled in first. He's not going anywhere."

"But—"

"No buts. You can freshen up. I don't want you going to see him in the state you're in. You're gonna have to calm down," he said sternly, "do you understand me?"

"Yes."

"Good. He doesn't need to see you this upset."

An hour later, Ethan took Toni to the jail to see Calvin. After checking in at the front desk, they were led down a hall to see Calvin. He stood up when she entered the visitation room. Although he'd told her not to fly to Detroit to see him, he was happy to see her. He watched anxiously as the guard pointed her in his direction and smiled when she turned and looked at him. The worried and confused look that she wore on her face didn't mask her angelic beauty. When she spotted Calvin standing behind the glass partition, she forced a nervous smile and walked over to him. He wanted to reach out and touch her but couldn't. Instead, he put the palm of his hand against the glass.

Toni put the palm of her hand against the glass where his was. The sight of him standing there in jail-issued attire gave her an overwhelming need to cry, but she fought it. Even though his otherwise-smooth face sported a day's worth of stubble, he was still as handsome as he was when she'd met him seven years ago.

"Calvin, what's going on?" she asked, but Calvin couldn't hear her.

He picked up his white phone and gestured for her to do the same.

Toni picked up her phone and brought it to her ear.

"Hey, babe." He smiled. "Go ahead and sit down."

They both sat.

"You look great, babe."

"Calvin," she whispered in a trembling voice. "What's going on?"

"I don't know, babe. It's just a case of mistaken identity is all I can think of. You know I didn't rape anybody. You believe me, don't you?"

"Yes, I believe you. I know you wouldn't do anything like that."

"But it doesn't look good for me. They got all this evidence against me. I look guilty as hell."

"I know." She stared at her husband and for the first time

in her life, she saw a vulnerable side to him. *He looks worried.*
"Ethan said you fired your lawyer—why?"

"Because I'm innocent, and I didn't think I needed him to
prove it. I figured the evidence would speak for itself."

"But the evidence is against you, Calvin. Everything's
falling apart. They said that girl won't change her story. She
still says it was you."

"I've never seen that girl before in my life, I swear." He
looked down at the table, took a deep breath, and then
looked back at his wife. "Toni, you know I haven't always
been faithful to you. You know I've slept around since we've
been together."

Hearing him say it somehow made it hurt even more, even
though Toni was aware of his cheating ways.

"But I've never forced anyone to do anything that they
didn't want to do."

"I know. You don't have to convince me, Calvin. Raping
someone is not in you."

"Thanks. Now if you could convince the police that I'm innocent then I'd be okay."

"What about the DNA test? Ethan said they did a DNA test
on you. That should remove all doubt."

"The police say that the DNA test takes a few days to complete. I go before the judge tomorrow. Maybe they'll set bail
so I can get the hell out of here."

"Well, I'm going to call that lawyer back. I'll tell him that
we really need him to take your case. He'll know what to do
to help you get out of this mess."

"That guy's not coming back, not after the way I—"

"Yes, he will. I'll tell him that you were under stress, that you didn't know what you were saying. He'll understand. I'm sure this type of stuff happens every day to him—he'll come back. And he'll be here tomorrow with you in court, and so will I." Toni forced a smile in an effort to comfort her husband.

"Thanks, Toni." He was happy to know she still had his back. She always had his back even though he put her through hell. "Is Ethan taking good care of you?"

"Yes. He's been my pillar through this; it's a good thing we have him."

"Does he believe I'm innocent?"

"Yes. He just wished he knew how he could help you better."

Chapter Twelve

After posting the one hundred thousand dollar bail that the judge set, Calvin was released. As soon as they returned home from Detroit, Calvin headed upstairs to take a shower while Toni went to check the messages on the answering machine.

The blinking message light informed her that they had twenty-three messages waiting. Knowing that they were probably all for, or about, Calvin, she decided to let him deal with them. As she started to head upstairs to join Calvin, the telephone rang. She checked the caller ID. It was one of her best friends, Jamise Taylor. She contemplated not answering the call. After the second ring, she picked up the receiver. "Hello."

"Trifling," was all Jamise said.

"What?"

"You are so trifling. My best friend's husband gets arrested for rape and I have to hear about it on the local news. What in the hell is wrong with you, girl? Why didn't you call me?"

"I didn't have time. I just got back in town from Detroit. I really just walked in the door."

"And your cell's not working? I've called you about ten times already."

"Girl, everybody's blowing my cell up, so I turned it off. My mom won't leave me alone."

"Well, you didn't tell her shit either. She told me she talked to you, but she still doesn't know anything. What the hell is going on?"

"I don't know. Some girl was raped in Detroit in the same hotel that Calvin was staying in. She says he did it, but it's obviously a mistake."

"So what did Calvin say about it?"

"He says he didn't do it, of course."

"And I bet you believe him, right?"

"Yes, I believe him. Calvin doesn't have to rape anyone."

"That's right—he doesn't have a problem getting other women to fuck him."

Toni knew what she was getting at and didn't want to go there with her. "Listen, Jamise, I'd—"

"No, Toni, you listen. Your mom's worried about you. Me and the girls are worried about you."

Toni sighed. She knew what was coming.

"Whether Calvin raped that girl or not, he still runs around on you—you need to leave his sorry ass."

"I'm not listening to this right now, okay?" Toni paced the floor.

"But he's a prick, Toni. He has no respect for you, no respect for your friends and family; he doesn't even try to hide his shit."

"If you keep bad-mouthing my husband, I'm gonna hang up."

"Okay, okay, okay." Jamise quickly changed her tone. She was sure that one phone call from her wasn't going to make Toni leave him now. However, she was hoping Toni would dump his sorry ass if they found out that Calvin did rape that girl. "Listen, girl, you know we love you and we want the best for you."

"I know."

"We're here for you, you know that?"

"Yeah, I know."

"If you need anything, I mean anything, you give us a call, okay?"

"I will."

"And you let us know what happens with Calvin too, okay?"

"I will."

"Promise?"

Toni smiled. "Promise."

"Okay, I love you, girl."

"Love you too."

After getting off the phone with Jamise, Toni hurried upstairs to find Calvin. He was still in the shower. Wanting to surprise him, she quickly stripped off her clothes and slipped into the bathroom. She pulled back the shower and stepped inside.

"What are you doing?" Calvin turned around and looked at her.

"I'm gonna take a shower." She smiled and moved toward him. She slipped her arms around him and gently covered his chest with wet kisses. Calvin became aroused as she pressed her body against his.

"Toni, we don't have a condom." He slipped his hands down over her wet ass and gently squeezed her.

"Don't worry, I have one right here." Her lips traveled down his chest and across his belly. His stomach tensed as she traced her tongue over his abs. Her hand slipped down over his swollen manhood to feel its hard thickness. She slowly stroked his penis, gently applying just enough pressure to push him to the next level.

Calvin began moving his hips forward, wanting more. Knowing this, Toni took him in her mouth. Calvin watched as she gently teased the head, causing barely audible moans to escape Calvin's lips. When he could take no more of her teasing, he pushed himself farther in her mouth. Toni began to nurse on him.

"Oh shit." Calvin quickened his pace.

She sucked, licked, and stroked to the point where he was about to explode.

"Oh, baby, I'm gonna cum," he moaned.

"No, not yet." She quickly slipped the condom on him and stood up.

He grabbed her, pushed her against the shower wall, and pulled one of her legs up and around his waist, entering her in one movement.

Toni gasped.

He grabbed her other leg and wrapped it around his waist, slipped his hands down over her buttocks and pushed himself deeper inside her. Once he had her secure in his grip, he began to thrust himself into the warm wet flesh of her womanhood.

Toni dug her nails into his back as she clung on to him. Their pace quickened as their bodies pounded against each other in heated passion.

"You gonna make me cum, Toni. Oh God, you gonna make me cum," he moaned against her ear as he felt himself about to erupt.

"Oh, Calvin." Toni climaxed in his arms.

Seconds later, he followed. But Calvin wasn't finished. He carried her out of the shower, poured her unto the bed, and ravaged her again.

Chapter Thirteen

The next morning, Calvin slipped out of bed and walked over to the bedroom window. "It's good to be home." He watched the press that had camped out on his front lawn. The reporters started showing up as soon as Calvin and Toni arrived home the night before. The day before it had only been a couple of journalists, but today there was a crowd of about twenty or more.

"It's good to have you home again." Toni smiled. She climbed out of bed and walked over to him. "Are they still out there?"

"Yep—a bunch of vultures just waiting to eat me alive."

"Hopefully, when they get the DNA results back and clear your name, they'll be outta our hair." She stepped up behind him and slipped her arms around his waist. "Come back to bed—last night was wonderful."

"I can't." He pushed her away and walked over to the nightstand. The day before he'd ignored the pesky reporters that had invaded their privacy in hopes that they would give up and just go home, but today, their persistence infuriated him. He opened the drawer and retrieved his Glock, checked to see if it was loaded, and then stuffed it in the back of his jeans.

"Calvin, what are you doing?"

"First, I'm gonna clean the shit off the lawn and then take a ride." He picked up his car keys from off the dresser and headed for the bedroom door.

Toni quickly followed him out the room and down the spiral staircase. "Are you trying to get yourself locked up again?" she asked, trying to keep up with him.

"Look, I've been accused of a crime I didn't commit, locked up for a crime I didn't commit. My entire tour has been cancelled because of a crime I didn't commit. The way I see it—I need to start breaking some laws to make up for lost time."

As he reached for the front door, Toni grabbed his arm. "Don't do this, Calvin," she pleaded. "I don't want you back in jail. Seeing—"

"Stand back." He pushed her away, pulled opened the front door, and looked out at the reporters.

"No."

When the reporters noticed Calvin standing at the front door, they began to rush toward him with cameramen in tow. "Mr. Wallace, Mr. Wallace," they called out.

Calvin reached behind his back and pulled out the gun from his waistband. Holding his Glock up, he aimed at the sky—"Get the fuck off my lawn, you sons of bitches!"—and fired into the air.

The sounds of reporters hounding him with questions were replaced with screams of fright, as the press scampered for shelter. As the crowd dispersed, Calvin walked over to his dark blue pearl Navigator, casually slipped inside, and pulled away.

Toni watched in silence as the reporters began to re-group.

"Did you get that?" one reporter asked her cameraman.

"Sure did. Every second of it." He smiled proudly.

"Mrs. Wallace, Mrs. Wallace." Some of them started toward her.

Disgusted by their behavior, Toni slammed the door in their faces. Not knowing what to do next, she paced her living room floor, pushing her hand through her hair. She stopped when she thought about Ethan. *Ethan would know what to do.* She raced to the phone and dialed his number.

"Hello," Ethan said.

"Ethan, it's me, Toni. I think he's gone crazy," she blurted out.

"Calm down, Toni." He could hear the desperation in her voice. "Tell me what happened."

She took a deep breath and tried to slow down. "Calvin just took off. There were reporters outside on the lawn. Calvin grabbed his gun, went out into the yard, and shot into the air. Then he jumped into his car and took off."

"Do you know where he went?"

"No. He said something about breaking the law. I'm scared he's gonna hurt somebody or get himself hurt. He's gonna get himself in more trouble."

"Listen, maybe he just needed to blow off some steam. I'll try to find him, okay?"

"Okay. What should I do?"

"Just sit tight; he might come back home. Call me if he does."

"All right."

He hung up the phone and slipped out of bed.

"Who was that?" Kenya asked, rolling over and looking at him. She watched as he pulled up his underwear and adjusted himself.

"That was my client's wife." Ethan grabbed his slacks and began slipping them on. "Her husband just took off, and she's worried about him."

"Ah, don't go." Kenya pulled back the covers to reveal her nakedness in an attempt to lure him back into her arms. "Come back to bed," she purred.

Calvin hesitated for a second or two to entertain the thought, but quickly pushed it out of his mind. Toni needed him a lot more than he needed another nut. "Sorry, Kenya, but I have to take care of this." He grabbed his shirt and slipped it on. "I will take a rain check, however." After giving her a quick kiss on the lips, he put on his shoes, grabbed his keys, and headed out to find Calvin.

A few hours later, after checking out all of the places that Calvin frequented, Ethan went over to check on Toni. He wasn't surprised to find a few diehard reporters still staking out the house. But they weren't at all interested in him; they were awaiting Calvin's return.

Ethan rang the doorbell.

Toni rushed down the stairs to see who it was. When she realized it was Ethan, she quickly opened up. "Did you find him?"

"No, I'm sorry. I guess you haven't heard from him either?"

"No. It's been four hours. Where can he be?"

"I have no idea. I've searched everywhere." He could tell

she was on the verge of tears. "Come here." He pulled her into his arms and held her. "He's gonna be okay, I promise you. He's got so much on his mind, so much to deal with right now. After he blows off some steam, he'll be back home, ready to deal with all this mess that he's going through."

Toni cried quietly in his arms. He held her so gently. In the seven years that she'd been with Calvin, he'd never held her like this, had never been so gentle.

Ethan slowly released her and took a step back. "Come on," he said. He placed his index finger on her chin and tilted her head up, forcing her to look up at him. "Let's go have a seat in the living room. I'll make you some coffee, and I'll stay here with you until he comes home, okay?"

Toni stared up at him. *Why couldn't Calvin be more like Ethan? Why didn't he possess the same kindness and gentleness?* She felt a closeness to him that she'd never felt with Calvin. She wanted to close her eyes, lay her head against his chest, and listen to the gentle beat of his heart. She wanted him to be Calvin.

Suddenly feeling guilty about their closeness, Toni stepped back to put more distance between them. She was a good woman, a faithful wife, and she knew that Ethan had a good heart. Even though Calvin had little, if any, respect for their marriage, she couldn't and wouldn't lower herself to his level. Nor would she ask Ethan to do the same.

"You don't have to stay."

"I know I don't have to—I want to. I don't want to leave you here alone worrying by yourself."

"You don't have to baby-sit me; I know you have other things to do."

"Maybe, but I'd rather be baby-sitting." Ethan smiled. "Now, how about I fix you some coffee?"

"Coffee sounds good."

"Good, now you go sit down, and I'll be with you in a minute."

"Okay."

A few hours later, after driving around aimlessly in an attempt to clear his head, Calvin arrived at the home of his good friend and fellow rapper, David. Originally from Richmond, Virginia, David Moore moved to Atlanta a year earlier with his wife and newborn daughter when he signed on with Southern Scope Records. Calvin and David met while working on their respective CD's. They fast became friends. Even though David's CD wasn't blowing up the way Calvin's was, they didn't allow that to affect their solid friendship.

Needing someone to talk to that was not directly affected by his situation, Calvin figured that David was the man. Calvin didn't have much family, and the family he did have always had their hands out asking for money. That same family stood by and watched his poor single mother struggle in the projects to raise him all by herself without so much as offering her a hand. To Calvin, David was the closest thing he had to family.

As he waited for David to answer the door, his cell phone rang. He figured it was Toni again, but when he looked at the caller ID, he realized that it was one of his so-called family members.

When news of the rape charges first surfaced, his so-called family was the first to call to see if they were true. Knowing that they really didn't give a damn about him, he ignored their calls, figuring they were just being nosy. He hadn't talked to any blood relatives since he was arrested, and he had no intentions of talking about or discussing his situation with them.

Just as Calvin locked his cell phone back onto his belt clip, David opened the door. Anxious to see a friendly face, Calvin looked at him and smiled. Much to his surprise, David just stared at him with a somber, almost bothered look on his face.

"Yo, man, what's up?"

"What's up?" It was evident from David's tone and the look on his face that he wasn't happy to see Calvin.

"Nothing, man." Calvin laughed, trying to lighten the mood.

David forced a smile. He'd learned about the rape charges against his buddy two days ago and wanted to go and talk to him, but once Traci—his wife—found out that Calvin was accused of sexual assault, she went on a bitching rampage. She let David know, in no uncertain terms, that she always thought Calvin was a piece of shit because of the way he treated Toni, as well as every other woman he came across. She also informed David that she didn't want Calvin anywhere near him or their daughter. Because of her obvious distaste for his friend, David avoided contacting him to keep the peace in his household. Now Calvin was standing on his doorstep, looking for a friendly face.

After a few seconds of staring each other down in uncomfortable silence, Calvin spoke up. "So what does a nigga have to do to get an invitation to come inside?" he asked in a nervous chuckle. It was apparent to him that he wasn't welcome, but he needed someone to talk to.

"Yo, man, I'm sorry." David laughed as he tried to play it off. "Where are my fuckin' manners? You know us niggas,

111

man—we ain't got no upbringing, and you know with us, you don't need an invitation. Come on in." He stepped back so Calvin could enter.

"Thanks, man." Calvin slipped inside, and David closed the door behind him. "I was a little worried, man, that I wasn't welcome anymore."

"Hell no, man, you know you're always welcome here. *Mi casa es su casa.*"

"Thanks, man." Calvin followed David into the den.

"No problem, dog. I'd expect the same from you." He walked over to the bar and fixed himself a drink. "So what you drinking?" he called over his shoulder as Calvin made himself comfortable on the leather couch.

"You know me, man."

"Hennessy?"

"Yeah."

After fixing the drinks, David walked over and handed Calvin his before sitting down across from him in the matching leather high-back chair.

"So what's up, man?"

"I'm in a whole hell of a lot of trouble—that's what up." Calvin sipped his drink.

"Oh yeah, man. I heard about that. I was gonna give you a call but—"

"Don't worry about it."—Calvin tried to prevent his friend from having to lie to him—"I know you're busy."

"So what are you going to do?"

"I don't know. I'm just waiting on the DNA result to clear me. I don't know what else to do." He took another swallow of his drink. "Yo, man, you got a joint; I could use a good hit right now."

"Naw, you know Traci don't allow that shit in here."

"Damn, man, it's your damn house. You paying the mutha-fuckin' mortgage on this big-ass bitch." Calvin looked around the room.

"Yeah, man, but with the baby and shit, I wait till I get out the house to do that shit."

"Pussy!" Calvin laughed.

"Yeah, I got your—" He stopped in mid-sentence as his wife stepped into the den with her three-year-old daughter on her hip—"Yo, baby, what's up?"

Traci didn't respond to her husband. She just stood there staring at the two men with obvious dissatisfaction written all over her face.

Calvin looked at her. *The beast from the east.* Traci was the kind of wife you didn't want. She was what Calvin termed, "on permanent PMS." And no matter how thuggish David portrayed himself in the hip-hop scene, it was apparent to Calvin that Traci was more of a thug than her husband. She was nothing like Toni. Toni was a lady. Traci was a straight-out-of-Compton bitch with a straight-out-of-Compton atti-tude to match. Unable to help himself, Calvin said, "What? You too good to speak?"

"David, I need to speak with you for a minute?"

David quickly glanced at Calvin and then back at his wife as he stood up. "Yeah, what's up?" He followed her outside the room but not out of earshot.

Calvin got up and fixed himself another drink as he lis-tened to their conversation. He felt it was only fair since he knew he was the topic of discussion.

"What the hell is he doing here?" Traci put her daughter down and ushered her away. She didn't want Kameron to hear the conversation; she had a feeling it was going to get heated.

"He just needed someone to talk to."

"Well I don't want him here, not in my house."

"Traci, he's our friend and he's in trouble."

"No—he was *your* friend and now he's a rapist."

"He says he didn't rape that girl."

"Yeah, like he's going to admit it. Get him out of here."

"Traci . . ."

"Get him out of here, David."

"And who the hell are you?"

Surprised by his response, she narrowed her eyes and glared at him. "I'm your muthafuckin' wife, bitch. And—"

"Bitch? You calling *me* a bitch? Girl, you better get the hell outta my face."

"Yeah, I'll get outta your face and take half of everything you got with me. I got my attorney on speed dial. Try me, nigga."

"Don't you threaten me, Traci."

"Then don't force my hand. I just simply asked you to get him the hell outta here. If his friendship means more to you than me and your daughter then—"

"Yo, David, I'm gonna head out." Calvin decided they'd already argued enough over him.

"Yo, man, you—"

"I wasn't trying to cause problems for you and wifey here." He glanced at Traci, her arms crossed and a get-the-hell-outta-my-house look on her face. He gave her a quick smile and then looked back at David. "Yo, man, when you marry your second wife, talk to me first about getting her to sign a prenup. Then you won't have to listen to this shit."

Traci snarled, "Fuck you, bitch!"

"You kiss your mama with that mouth." Calvin laughed as he walked toward the front door.

David shot Traci a pissed-off look as he walked Calvin to the door. "I'm sorry, man."

"No problem. But damn! I didn't know Traci had a mouth like that on her—you need to put a muzzle on that shit."

"Yeah, I'll pick up one from the pet store."

"All right, I'll holler at you later, man."

"Do that."

As Calvin stood outside the closed door of his friend's house, he could hear the screams coming from inside. He knew they'd be arguing for days over this one since Traci never let shit go and David was still trying to play the man, even though it was evident that he was Traci's bitch.

He pushed his hand through his hair as he thought about his situation. He needed two things—to get fucked and to get fucked up.

Chapter Fourteen

After leaving David's, Calvin made a couple of stops to pick up a few items that would help him complete one half of his mission—to get fucked up. To accomplish the second half of his mission, he knew exactly where to go.

He ended up at Bottom's Up, a local strip club, and found himself on the receiving end of a lap dance. As he sat leaned back on a plush black velvet couch in the champagne room, he watched as Milk Chocolate danced provocatively in front of him, wearing nothing but a G-string.

"Make it clap for me," Calvin mumbled as he slid the palm of his hand over her smooth, thick, round ass.

Without saying a word, she turned around, giving him full access to her ass, leaned forward and bounced, making her ass cheeks slap together.

Calvin licked his lips and grinned as he watched her glistening ass cheeks jiggle to the beat of the music in the background. His already throbbing dick ached to slip in between the two globes wiggling in front of him. He imagined himself sliding in and out of her wet hole. Unable to contain himself any longer, he grabbed her by the hips and pulled her to him as he buried his face between her ass cheeks. He inhaled deeply, taking in the scent of her wet, sweaty pussy.

"Hmm," he moaned. He loved the smell of pussy. The scent drove him crazy. So crazy, he couldn't resist the urge to stick out his tongue and probe her swollen mound.

Milk Chocolate moaned as his eager tongue tried to enter her pussy. She leaned over more, giving him more access to entrance.

He hooked his finger in the crotch of her G-string and pulled it aside, giving him full view of her pink, wet insides.

"Damn," he muttered just before slipping his tongue into her pussy. The distinct taste of her sweat and pussy juices drove him crazy. Calvin quickly fumbled with his pants as he tried to pull out his throbbing dick. He wanted to do more than just eat her. He wanted to fuck her.

In an attempt to assist her customer, Milk Chocolate reluctantly pulled away from his mouth, turned around, and kneeled down before him. She quickly finished undoing his pants, pushed them along with his boxers down, and released his swollen cock. Without hesitation, she took him in her mouth and began sucking vigorously.

Calvin watched as the stripper nursed on his shaft. He thrust his hip forward as he tried to push himself deeper into her mouth.

"That's right—slob it down," he moaned as her spit spilled out of her mouth and down the length of him. He could tell she was a pro the way his head slipped down into her throat. "Damn," he mumbled to himself as he thought about his wife. Toni could never do any shit like that. "Oh shit, I'm gonna cum." He grabbed the back of her head and pushed her down further on his dick. She soon began gagging, but he wouldn't let up. "You can do it," he moaned just before he shot off down her throat. Only after emptying himself completely inside her, did he let her go.

Milk Chocolate fell onto the floor, clutching at her throat with her hand as she coughed and gasped for air. "You sick bastard," she yelled at him after she finally caught her breath.

"Aw, you know you loved it." He smiled, refastened his pants, and stood up to leave.

Calvin slipped into the front seat of his Navigator. He pulled out a joint and lit it up. After he took a hit, he opened the bottle of Jim Bean, brought it to his lips, and took a swallow. "Ahhh," he said as the liquor went down. He took another hit off the joint and sat back to wait for it to take effect.

R. Kelly and Ron Isley's song, "Down Low," was playing on the radio. The lyrics caught his attention, and he turned up the volume. The story of a young woman cheating on her husband made him think of Toni and Ethan. Was he imagining things, or were they getting closer? He trusted Toni and knew that she would never step out on him, and he trusted Ethan too.

Even though Ethan was his manager, he also considered him a friend. But Calvin had noticed the way he looked at Toni and after the comment he made about Toni back in Detroit, he was beginning to wonder if he had a thing for his wife. He sat there contemplating the relationship between his wife and his manager and began to worry. Now he felt a sudden urge to go home and confront his wife and see what the hell was going on with her and his manager.

* * *

Hours later, Toni and Ethan were still waiting for Calvin's return home. Toni, already upset because of the way he took off, was beginning to panic because they still hadn't heard from him. If it wasn't for Ethan's cool head, she would have lost it hours ago. "Maybe we should try the police station again. Maybe they've picked him up." She paced the floor; she didn't know what else to do.

"They said they would call us if they heard anything; besides, he's not really missing, he just needed to blow off some steam." He hated to see her going through this. He knew that Calvin was stressed out because of the situation, but to take off for so long, having his wife worrying about him like this was ridiculous.

But he wasn't surprised by Calvin's desertion. This was just like him, not worrying about anybody else except himself. All Calvin had to do was pick up a phone and call Toni to let her know he was okay.

"It's almost eleven," Ethan said as he glanced at his watch. "Why don't we check out the local news to see if there is any new development?"

"I'm just so tired of seeing them persecuting my husband in the media." Toni stopped pacing. "They've already tried and convicted him."

"We know the truth, Toni—we know he couldn't do anything like that."

"I know. Thanks for being here." She looked up at him.

"Come on," he said as he slipped his hand in hers and led her to the sofa.

Toni turned on the television to catch the eleven o'clock news. She and Ethan weren't surprised to see her husband as the lead story for the third day in a row:

*Hip-hop's newest bad boy has just gotten worse. This was the
scene earlier today at the Wallaces' home . . ."*

As the video ran, the reporter continued to comment:

*Rap star, Calvin Wallace, aka Blayze, stepped out of his
front door this morning waving his gun. He shot into the air
as he demanded that reporters leave his home.*

*Three days ago, the rap star was charged with rape and ag-
gravated assault against a Detroit woman. Although he denies
any involvement in the assault, there is evidence to the contrary.*

*In addition, as if things couldn't get worse for Mr. Wallace,
we've also learned that three days ago he assaulted the DJ at
WFUK radio station during an interview to promote his concert. We are still waiting to see if he will be charged.*

*Needless to say, the tour to help promote his triple platinum
CD has been cancelled indefinitely. Although the DA feels that
the State has an airtight case against Mr. Wallace, they are
still waiting for the results of the DNA test before they indict
him.*"

"Can this get any worse?" Toni looked over at Ethan.

"It will get better." Ethan slid over next to her, put his arm
on her shoulder, and pulled her next to him. She rested her
head on his chest and cried lightly.

Minutes later, he could tell she had fallen asleep as her
body relaxed against him and her breathing became heavier.
He pulled her a little closer and ran his fingers through her
hair. *It felt good to hold her like this. If Calvin knew what he had in
her, he wouldn't treat her like shit. He wouldn't be running around*

fucking all these other women. He'd be home making love to her every night. Ethan told himself if he ever got the chance to love her, he would love her forever.

Unable to help himself, he leaned over and gently kissed her forehead. He closed his eyes, as his lips remained pressed against her skin. She took his breath away. Then, feeling guilty for his actions, he pulled his lips away from her and vowed never to cross that line with her again. Trying to get her out of his head, he turned his attention back to the television and continued watching the local news.

After successfully managing to arrive home safely without ending up in an accident, a drunken Calvin stumbled out of his car. The reporters that had trampled his once manicured lawn and surrounded his home earlier that day had disappeared.

As he made his way toward his house, he noticed Ethan's car parked in his driveway. This only fueled his already suspicious feelings.

"Sorry muthafuckas," he growled. He glanced at his watch. Here it was 1:30 in the morning and this muthafucka was hanging around his house, fucking his wife. *Somebody is going to die tonight.* Feeling betrayed by both his wife and his manager, he reached behind him and pulled out his Glock that he had tucked in his waistband.

He made his way toward the house, stopped at the front door, and listened as if he half-expected to hear his manager fucking his wife. When all he heard was silence, he unlocked the door and stumbled inside. Once inside, he could hear the TV on in the living room. He made his way toward the sound. He entered the den to find Ethan holding Toni on the sofa. He stumbled toward them.

"Don't you two look nice and cozy," he said, his speech a little slurred.

Ethan turned around to see him standing there waving his Glock. He gently nudged Toni to awaken her.

She looked up at him, and when Ethan nodded his head in Calvin's direction, she turned and looked at him. "Calvin." She pulled herself away from Ethan, and they both stood up.

"You two could have at least waited until they locked me up." Calvin moved toward them, still holding his gun out.

"I was just comforting her," Ethan tried to explain; "she was worried about you." He kept his eyes glued on the gun. He didn't want Calvin to do anything stupid.

"You see, Ethan, you're a man; I can understand why you couldn't wait, but Toni . . . I expected more from you. I didn't expect you to start fuckin' my manager until they locked me up." He chuckled. "I guess I was wrong about you. You're no different than those ho's I fuck in the street."

"Calvin, we weren't—"

"At least with the ho's in the streets, you know they're ho's. I thought you were a lady—I guess I was wrong about that."

"Calvin, give me the gun." Ethan pushed Toni behind him and took a step toward Calvin. "You're just upset; you don't know what you're saying."

"Ha!" Calvin pointed the gun towards them. "See, you're wrong. I know what I'm saying. I just said my wife was a ho. See there." He stumbled to the side as he started to shake the gun at him. "You think I'm drunk, don't you?"

"Calvin, please . . ." Toni begged, ". . . please give Ethan the gun."

Ignoring his wife's pleas, he continued. "She's good, isn't she? Nobody can suck a dick the way my wife can suck a dick. Has she sucked yours yet?"

"Calvin, there's nothing going on between me and Toni. Now give me the gun, and then we'll put you to bed." Ethan took another step toward him.

"Fuck you, nigga—oh my bad, my wife's already fuckin' you."

"The only fuckin' going on around here is you fuckin' up your life over this bullshit."

"You're right, this is nothing but bullshit," he agreed. Calvin finally lowered his gun. "I didn't rape nobody. I never touched that girl. You believe me, don't you?" He forgot about the gun and focused more on convincing them that he wasn't a rapist.

Ethan saw an opportunity to get the gun away from him. He cautiously moved toward him. "Of course, we believe you. Toni and I know you wouldn't do any shit like that. We are here to support you." Slowly he reached for the gun as he continued to talk. "We know that you are going through a whole lot of shit." Ethan's fingers finally felt the cold steel of the gun barrel. "I don't blame you for being upset, man." He curled his fingers around the barrel as he tried to get a good grip without alarming Calvin. "But you know how much Toni loves you, don't you?"

Once he had secured a tight grip, he slowly slipped the gun from Calvin's hand. He slid the gun behind his back so Toni could get it. Once he felt her take possession of the weapon, he brought both hands back to Calvin to help steady him. "You do know how much your wife loves you, don't you?" he repeated.

"Yes." Calvin struggled to stand still.

"Put that away," Ethan instructed Toni as he held Calvin up.

Toni knew just the place to hide the gun so he couldn't get to it. She immediately raced out of the living room, through the kitchen, and into the garage, where her Jaguar was parked.

"And you know that I'm your boy, right?" Ethan tried to assure Calvin. "You know I would never fuck over you?"

"You my nigga," Calvin said.

"Then let's squash this shit right now, all right?"

Calvin clumsily nodded in agreement. "All right."

"So it's squashed?"

"It's squashed. You my nigga, man." He stumbled again.

"That's right, I'm your nigga, your boy, your right-hand man. I would never fuck with your woman, man."

"That's right, or I'd have to kill you, nigga." Calvin chuckled.

After securing the gun in the trunk of her Jaguar, she hurried back to the living room. "I locked it up," she told Ethan.

"Good. Now help me get him to bed."

Toni slipped Calvin's arm over her shoulder as she wrapped her arm around his waist; Ethan did the same on the other side. The two of them struggled to get him up the spiral staircase and into their bedroom. They carried him over to the bed and laid him face up.

"Ménage à trois," Calvin said when Toni started undoing his pants and Ethan removed his shoes.

"No," an embarrassed Toni said as she pushed his roaming hand away after he started squeezing her breast.

"I love your tits." He laughed drunkenly and clumsily reached for them again.

"Stop." She shoved his hands away. She was disgusted by the way he was fondling her in front of his manager. Feeling Ethan's eyes on her as her husband tried to feel her up, Toni made it a point to keep her head down in hopes that Ethan wouldn't see how repulsed and embarrassed she was.

Equally disturbed by the way Calvin was groping her, and feeling her obvious humiliation, Ethan tried to discourage him. "Come on, man, you've got no time for that. You have to get some sleep." He began to help Toni remove Calvin's pants.

As they worked to lower his jeans, they noticed red lipstick on his briefs and thighs. The sight of this made Toni stop and step back. Anger and disgust welled up inside her, tears formed in her eyes.

Ethan looked over at Toni. "Damn," he muttered when he saw her pain.

Toni shook her head in disbelief.

"Toni," Ethan whispered.

She continued shaking her head and began backing away from them. She didn't know how much more of this she could take.

Ethan tried again. "Toni."

Toni ran out of the bedroom and raced downstairs with Ethan following.

When he got downstairs, he found her sitting in the living room crying. Ethan kneeled down in front of her. "Are you okay?" He stared up at her tiny face.

Trying to gather her wits, Toni quickly wiped the tears away. She was ashamed to cry like that in front of Ethan. "I'm fine." She nodded as she tried to avoid his probing eyes.

"Why do you expect more from him?"

"I don't know." She finally made eye contact with him. "I guess I was just hoping that with everything that was going on, that he'd give up the other women for a while."

"You deserve so much better than this—don't you see that?"

"But I love him."

"I know." Ethan stared up at her large brown eyes. *I could love you so easily.* He wanted to kiss her, to tell her everything he was feeling inside, but he had vowed not to ever cross the line with her again. Earlier, it was just a kiss on her forehead, but right now, it could be so much more. He knew his feelings for her were dangerous, especially since she had an unpredictable gun-wielding husband.

"You should go home," Toni said, breaking the silence.

"I don't mind staying." Ethan's cell phone rang. "Excuse me." He pulled it out and checked the caller ID. "It's Kenya—I better take it." He stood up and stepped away from Toni so he could have some privacy. "Hello."

After the brief conversation with Kenya, he hung up his cell and walked back over to where Toni was. "Sorry about that."

"No problem. You have to go?"

"No, she'll be okay."

"Listen, your woman's calling you. I'm okay. Go home and take care of business; I know you have a life outside the Wallaces." She smiled. "Besides, if you were my man, I wouldn't want to take second chair to another man's wife."

"Are you sure you're gonna be okay and you don't mind me leaving?

"No, I don't mind. You can't sit here holding my hand all day. You really should go home."

"You don't mind me leaving, but are you going to be okay?" He was worried about what Calvin might do if he woke up. "I really don't like the idea of you being here alone with him; he might try to hurt you or something."

"I'll be fine."

"What about the gun?—are you sure you hid it somewhere where he won't be able to get to it?"

"I locked it in the trunk of my car. Besides, Calvin's out cold, and he'll probably be out the rest of the night. He won't give me any trouble until tomorrow."

"And you'll give me a call if you need me."

"I promise. Now go home."

"Only if you're sure." He searched her eyes for reassurance.

She smiled. "I'm sure." Although she truly wanted him to stay and hold her hand, she knew he couldn't put his life on hold for her or Calvin, and she wasn't going to ask him to.

"If you insist."

"I insist." She walked him to the front door.

Just before leaving, he turned around and looked down at her. "If anything comes up, you give me a call."

"Okay." She nodded.

"Promise?"

"I promise."

"Okay." Reluctantly he left.

Still upset by her husband's blatant disregard for her feelings while she was trying her best to support him, Toni decided to spend the night in the guest bedroom. She didn't want to be anywhere near him tonight.

After leaving Toni, Ethan called Kenya back and told her she could meet him at his place. When he reached his apartment, she was already waiting for him in the parking lot.

As soon as they were in his apartment, Kenya was already stripping his clothes off. After she pulled his shirt off over his head, she pushed him down on the bed and straddled him. She leaned forward and covered his mouth with hers as he unfastened her blouse and peeled it from her body. Feeling his full hardness pressing between the warm eagerness of her womanhood, Kenya pulled her lips from his, slid back, giving her full access to his pants, and unfastened them. She smiled when she pulled out his swollen manhood that she was aching to have inside her. She slipped him in her mouth.

Ethan watched in amazement as her tongue and lips teased the swollen head. As she began to nurse more vigorously, he studied her technique as he remembered Calvin's words. "Nobody could suck a dick like my wife." He wondered if this was what it felt like to be in Toni's mouth. Then he quickly pushed her out of his thoughts. He closed his eyes and enjoyed the pleasure Kenya was providing him.

Realizing Ethan was primed for a mind-blowing fuck, Kenya stood up and removed the rest of her clothes. She climbed back on top of Ethan and slowly lowered herself on his throbbing shaft. She moaned as she felt the thickness of him filling her up.

Ethan gently took hold of her full hips and helped guide her up and down. "Oh, baby." He watched himself, glistening from her juices and disappearing inside of her repeatedly.

Kenya leaned forward and whispered in his ear. "You like that, baby?"

"Oh yeah, Toni, your pussy feels so good." Ethan gripped her hips even tighter.

"What?" Kenya stopped riding him. "What the hell did you just call me?"

Damn, Ethan mumbled to himself when he realized his mistake.

Before he could answer, Kenya had already dismounted him and was getting dressed.

He quickly sat up and reached for her. "Baby—"

"I can't believe this shit!" She quickly stepped out of his reach. "I can't believe this fuckin' shit."

"Toni, don't—" He slipped again. "Fuck! I mean, Kenya." He climbed out of bed.

"You are unbelievable! You are so fuckin' unbelievable!"

"It was a mistake." He tried to calm her down and reached for her again.

"Don't you dare touch me, you sorry piece of shit!"

There was no way to explain calling her by another woman's name. What was he going to tell her? He was fucking her, but was in love with his client's wife. He sat back down on the bed and put his head in his hands.

Seconds later, he heard his front door slamming closed behind Kenya as she left in tears.

Chapter Fifteen

The next day, Toni busied herself with errands while Calvin slept. Although she was furious with his behavior, she had to remain the good and faithful wife. She had to show her support for her husband and her belief in his innocence. Everybody had to know that she was going to stand by his side no matter how guilty he looked. And if it meant continuing to put up with his cheating ways, then she would do it.

After she picked up her dry cleaning, she glanced at her watch. It was nearing 2:00 in the afternoon. Wondering if he was awake yet, she decided to return home and check on him. When she reached their bedroom, he still lay there with his pants pushed halfway down, revealing the lipstick that sent her away crying the night before. *This time I'm not going to run away crying.* She walked over to the bed and stood over him. *No, Calvin didn't have to rape anyone. Women sucked and fucked him on their own free will.*

She leaned over and studied his face. He was a good-looking man. She couldn't deny that. He also had a well-maintained physique and was worth a shitload of money. She understood why the women couldn't resist him. She had found him irresistible for the past seven years. She smiled slightly as she brought her hand up and traced her finger over the smooth brown skin of his chin. As she marveled at its soft strength, she allowed her fingertips to travel over his full lips, to the tip of his strong nose and then over his forehead. She leaned in a little closer and brought her lips to his ear. "You lousy son of a bitch," she whispered.

Meanwhile in Detroit, Detective Vinson walked over to Crowder's desk as she finished up some paperwork.

"So what's up?" she asked as he made himself comfortable on the edge of her desk.

"Something just doesn't sit right with me on the Waters' case." Vinson held up the hotel brochure.

"What about it?"

"This guy's action doesn't make sense to me. I mean, he rapes a woman in an elevator of a busy hotel where could easily get caught. She was on her way up to his room, but he attacks before he gets there."

"Maybe he didn't want to mess up his room or leave any evidence."

"Then why did he rape her in an elevator that has surveillance cameras installed? Look"—He handed her the brochure.

"What am I looking for?" Crowder glanced over it.

"Stapler said that security is important to their hotel and this rape is getting them bad press. So I studied the brochure—they advertise their surveillance cameras in their elevator to give their patrons a sense of security. So why would Calvin Wallace, a big-name rap star with a highly recognizable face, rape a woman in front of a video camera?"

"Maybe he's dumb as hell." She tossed the brochure on the pile of paper that covered her desk.

"Then there are his hands. You saw the videotape. He wasn't wearing gloves. He beat that girl with his bare hands. How did he hit her that many times, that hard, and not have any injuries to his hands?"

"Search me."

"You sound like you don't care."

"I don't," she said as she stood up. "What I do care about is a nineteen-year-old girl that was beaten within inches of her life, then raped and humiliated. What I care about are women who find themselves helpless and at the mercy of some high-strung, egotistical rap star who thinks that he can do whatever the hell he wants and get away with it—that is what I care about." She crossed her arms and stared up at him.

"So you don't like hip-hop, huh?" he laughed.

"Yeah, yeah, yeah." She smiled as she unfolded her arms. Just then, her phone rang. "Hello."

Vinson stood up and was about to leave when she signaled him to wait.

A few seconds later, she hung up the phone and looked at her partner. "That was the lab with the results from the DNA tests."

"What's the verdict?"

"His DNA matches the DNA from the victim's rape kit."

"He did it?"

"Yep, but there's more."

"What else?"

"Check this out—the lab also recovered saliva from the victim and it was processed along with the semen. Like I said, the DNA of the semen matches that of Wallace, but the DNA from the saliva doesn't. The saliva is from a woman."

"A woman?"

"Yep, a woman. And it's not Tamela's either. I think we need to give her a visit," Crowder said; "I have a few more questions for her."

"Yeah, let's talk to her before we contact the DA about indicting him. We don't want any surprises that could get this guy off."

An hour later, Sean called out for Tamela as he closed the front door behind the detectives. "Have a seat," he said as he gestured toward the sofa.

Vinson sat down while Crowder remained standing. She strolled around the room, looking at photos on the wall.

When Tamela didn't appear, Sean excused himself while he went to get her. "Baby, the police are here to talk to you. They say they have a few more questions."

She looked up at him from her magazine. Her face still bore the signs of a savage attack. "More questions?" she repeated, trying to move her lips as little as possible. The slightest movement reminded her of the beating she took because of the pain. But she didn't need her lips to remind her; the constant aching of her face and head was reminder enough.

"Yeah, baby." Sean moved to the side of the bed. "They say they won't take up much time."

"Okay." Tamela carefully slid out of bed with his help. He

gently guided her down the hallway and into the living room. Tamela forced a weak smile and took a seat. Sean sat next to her on the arm of her chair.

Crowder turned her attention from the photos on the wall to Tamela as she walked over to where she was sitting. She sat down next to Vinson. "We didn't want to disturb you, but we have a few more questions before we go to the DA."

Tamela nodded.

"We just got the DNA results back from your rape kit, and the DNA matches that of Calvin Wallace."

"Good," Sean said. "Now throw that bastard in jail." He looked down at Tamela and then at the detectives.

"Well, when they tested the DNA, they also found DNA from the saliva of a woman. Can you explain?"

Tamela didn't answer, but the nervous look on her face was visible to both detectives.

"Miss Waters," Crowder said, "are you okay?"

"Yes," she muttered. "My feet are cold." She looked up at her boyfriend. "Sean, could you bring me my yellow slippers? They're in the bedroom closet."

"Sure, babe." Sean stood up and disappeared down the hallway.

Tamela turned her attention back to the detectives. "I'm sorry—I didn't want Sean to hear."

"Hear what?"

"I'm bisexual. I was with a woman before the attack. Sean doesn't know."

The detectives looked at each other and back at Tamela. "I understand," Crowder said. "Can you give us her name?"

"I'd rather not; I don't want to get her involved in all of this."

"But we are going to need her name to—" Vinson started to say.

"You don't need her for this. She's married, has kids—why drag her into all of this? Why ruin her life for that bastard who attacked me? You have what you need. You have the DNA and the tape and my testimony."

Crowder looked at Vinson. "The DA can get a conviction with what we have."

"Then how do we explain the saliva?" Vinson asked.

"I refuse to give you her name. I'm not getting her involved." She swallowed hard. "I'll lie."

"Tamela, if the DA prosecutes this, it's going to come out that you're bisexual," Crowder informed her.

"Maybe," she said. "Then my life will be ruined. But I refuse to destroy everything she has because of this; she didn't ask for this."

"I found them," Sean announced as he re-entered the living room. "They weren't in the closet though. I found them under the bed." He kneeled down in front of Tamela and began to slip them on her feet.

"Thanks, baby." She looked down at him and then up at the detectives. She was hoping they'd let it go.

"Tamela—" Vinson began, but Crowder quickly grabbed his arm.

"I think we have everything we need," Crowder said as she stood up. Following her lead, Vinson rose to his feet.

"Thank you." Tamela forced a weak smile, knowing Crowder let her off the hook.

"No problem." Crowder nodded.

"So what's going on with the saliva?" Sean asked after he finished slipping the bedroom shoes on his girlfriend's feet.

"We got it straightened out." Crowder told him as she and detective Vinson walked towards the front door.

After the detectives left, Tamela looked up at her boyfriend. "Sean . . ." she hesitated and then continued, "there's something I need to tell you."

A few hours later, back in Atlanta, Calvin swallowed a few aspirins in an attempt to get rid of his throbbing headache brought on by the drinking from the night before. "Thanks," he said to Toni as he handed her the empty water glass back.

She took the glass and turned to leave.

He grabbed her wrist, pulling her back to him. "Why you so quiet?—what did I do this time?"

"Just being you, Calvin; just being you." She tried to pull away from him, but he tightened his grip and pulled her closer, slipping his other arm around her waist. "I don't have time for games." She tried to pry herself free. "Besides, I thought you had a headache."

"Sex is good for a headache." Still holding her captive in his arm, he let go of her wrist and slipped his free hand up under her mini-skirt.

"Not now, Calvin. I'm not in the mood." She pushed his hand away.

"Come on, Toni. I need some loving." He took the glass from her and sat it on the nightstand.

"Then why don't you go back to that ho you fucked last night and get some?"

"I don't want her, I want you." He pulled her down on the bed and then rolled over on top of her.

"Calvin, let me up," she said just before he covered her mouth with his.

He kissed her hard as his hand slipped up under her skirt again and started trying to push her panties down. She used one hand to hold onto her underwear and the other to try to push him off her, all the while clenching her lips and teeth together to prevent his probing tongue from thrusting into her mouth. Then finally, she managed to turn her head and free her lips from her husband's. His mouth quickly traveled down to her neck where he began to suck vigorously.

She winced at the pain. "Calvin let me up!" she yelled, as she continued to struggle against him.

He pulled his mouth from her neck, raised himself up, and looked down at her. "Who are you fuckin'?"

"What?"

"Who are you fuckin'?—Ethan?"

She stared up at him in disbelief. She'd only been with one man her entire life and that was her husband. And now he had the balls to accuse her of sleeping with another man. After all the whoring around that he did, he had the nerve to accuse her of being unfaithful. She could barely believe he was asking her this.

"Are you fuckin' Ethan?" he yelled when she didn't respond.

"No!" she screamed as she tried to shove him off her.

"We'll see." He grabbed both of her hands and held them above her head. After securing both of her wrists in one of his hands, he reached down and hiked her skirt up.

"Calvin, no." She shook her head and stared up at him. *He couldn't be serious about this.*

"You're fuckin' someone." He began pushing her panties down again.

138

"Stop it!" She tried to squirm away from him.

"Is it Ethan? You giving it to Ethan?"

"No!" she screamed. "Calvin, please . . ."

Growing tired of her resistance, he stopped trying to push her panties down and ripped them away from her body instead.

"No! Calvin, stop!" She squeezed her legs together, but it was useless. "I'm not doing anything . . . I promise."

"I'll know in a minute," he hissed. With his free hand, he pried one of her legs from the other, just wide enough for him to wedge one of his knees between them. Then he slipped his other knee between them and pushed them further apart. He used his legs to hold them open as he pushed down his boxers to reveal his swollen manhood.

Think, think, Toni told herself as he tried unsuccessfully to enter her. "Condoms," she yelled out in an attempt to stop him. "You don't have on a condom." She prayed that this would stop him because he didn't believe in going in raw for fear that he would get her pregnant.

But Calvin was determined to have her right then and there, and using a condom was the last thing on his mind. He tried to enter her again, and she screamed out in pain as his invading manhood tore the skin of her entrance.

She tried to shift her body to get away from him, but it only made the pain worse.

"Whose pussy is this?" He shoved the rest of himself inside her.

Toni closed her eyes as he pushed her legs even farther apart so he could go deeper. Crying silently, she stopped fighting and tried to let her body relax as he began pumping every inch of himself inside her. When he noticed her resistance fade, he released her hands, lowered the rest of his body down on top of hers, and buried his face in the crook of her neck, where his mouth began to suck furiously, causing her more pain.

It's only sex, Toni tried to convince herself. *He's your husband and he's only having sex with you. Get over it.* But she couldn't get over it. Tears seeped from under her closed eyelids and ran down both sides of her face as her husband continued his assault on her.

Then as quickly as the assault began, it was over. Calvin climaxed and, instead of rolling off of her, he remained on top of her with his head buried against her neck as he waited to regain his energy. As his breathing began to return to normal, he could hear Toni crying beneath him. The sound of her sobbing brought him to the realization of what he'd just done. Instantly regretting his attack on his wife, he raised his head and stared down at her tear-covered face.

"Damn, baby, I'm sorry," he whispered.

She quickly turned her head and looked away at the wall. She didn't want to see him. She was too angry and hurt to look at him.

"Toni." He pushed her hair back away from her face and attempted to kiss away her tears.

"No," she mumbled as she shoved him off of her. She leaped from the bed, raced into the bedroom, and locked the door. Distraught by Calvin's attack, she slid down the wall onto the floor, pulled her knees to her chest, and cried.

Calvin's first instinct was to go after her, but he decided against it. He needed to figure out what in the hell was going on. He sat up on the edge of the bed. "Shit!"

In the seven years he had been with Toni, he'd never hurt her like that, never raised his hand to her, never threatened her. He may have been disrespectful and unfaithful, but he had never hurt her physically.

What in the hell is going on? What am I doing? Is it the pressure of the charges, or am I so jealous of the relationship she and Ethan had? Maybe it was both.

Toni sat in the bathroom floor wondering if she pushed him too far, if it was her actions that drove him to this point. She knew he was no angel, but she'd never feared for her safety until he was charged with rape. First, he pulled the gun on her and Ethan the night before, and now this.

Am I to blame? As she struggled to come to terms with what he'd just done to her, she heard the telephone ring.

Calvin's first thought was to ignore the call. He looked over at the caller ID and saw the number to Joseph's law firm. "Hey, Joseph, what's up?" he said, attempting to sound casual. He wondered how Toni was doing. He hoped he hadn't hurt her too much.

"Calvin, I need you to be totally honest with me about your relationship with Tamela Waters," Joseph said.

"There was no relationship."

"If I'm going to have any chance of getting you off, you have level with me. Did you rape that girl?"

"Hell no. How many times do I have to tell you I didn't touch her?"

"Do you know her?"

"Never saw her before they showed me the pictures."

"Then how can you explain them finding your semen inside her?"

"What? What the hell are you talking about?"

"The DA just called. The DNA results are back, and your semen matches the DNA of the semen found on the victim."

"No way," he insisted. "There's no fuckin' way there's a match! No fuckin' way!"

"Calvin," Joseph said, "if you know this girl—"

"I don't know her!"

"If you had sex with her before she was raped."

"I told you I never touched that girl! What the fuck is going on? Don't you hear me? Does anybody fuckin' hear me?"

"I can't help you if—"

"Joseph, you've got to fix this. There's no way I'm going to jail for this shit, do you hear me?"

"Listen, Calvin—"

"Hell no, *you* listen!—I didn't do this shit, and I'm not going down for it! So you make it go away!"

"I can't. If you slept with this girl—"

"What in the hell do I have to do? I didn't fuck that girl! I didn't rape that girl! Now fix it, damn it!" He slammed the receiver down. Calvin paced back and forth like a caged animal. *This couldn't be happening. How in the hell could this be happening?*

Toni sat in the bathroom listening to Calvin's conversation. She could tell by his response that it wasn't good news. Forgetting about his attack on her, and determined to show him that she was still going to stand by him, she quickly rose to her feet, opened the bathroom door, and watched him.

Calvin stopped and looked at her, when he noticed her standing there. He didn't know what to say to her. After what he had just done to her, how could he expect her to continue to stand by and support him?

"What is it?"

"Baby," he said staring at her, trying to figure out how to get the words out, "that was Joseph. He said that the DNA from that girl matched mine."

"No," she whispered as she shook her head and brought her hand to her mouth.

"I don't know how. I didn't rape that girl, Toni. I never touched that girl."

"Oh God, Calvin." She rushed over to him and hugged him.

"Baby, I never touched her. You gotta believe me." He held onto her.

"I believe you," she whispered against his chest. It was the first time since his mother passed away two years ago that she saw him hurting and scared. "I'll always believe you."

Chapter Sixteen

A few days later, Calvin, accompanied by his wife, his attorney, and his manager, sat in the back of a limousine, in front of a Detroit courthouse.

"Listen, Calvin," Joseph said, "they definitely have enough evidence to indict you, so don't be surprised if they do. They've tested the DNA twice at my request, and both came back as a match. They've got you on video, the victim's ID, and testimony. There is pretty much nothing we can do but show up, be courteous, and respect the court."

As Joseph's words trailed off, Calvin stared out of the window at the mob that crowded the streets and the courthouse steps. While some of the crowds were reporters aching to get a story, or die-hard fans showing their support, the vast majority of the crowds were protesters, mainly women who were either rape victim advocates or rape survivors themselves.

How in the hell did I wind up here? Calvin watched the heated faces and listened to the angry chants of the mob. *What have I done in life to deserve this?* He sat back and closed his eyes. He needed a joint to calm his nerves. Just one hit and he would be okay.

"Calvin, whatever you do, do not lose your temper. We don't need to give them any more ammunition," Joseph reminded him.

"Yeah, yeah," he answered without opening his eyes.

Toni reached over and slipped her hand in his. She half-expected him to pull away, but he didn't. Instead, he curled his fingers around hers and squeezed gently. He was scared and she knew it.

Ethan watched as Calvin held Toni's hand for the first time in his presence. He felt a twinge of jealousy but quickly pushed it aside. *She is off-limits.* Ethan also felt a little nervous about his role in front of the Grand Jury today. He knew that they were going to ask him about his inability to locate Calvin that night.

Even though Calvin had sworn that he was in his room the entire night, Ethan would have to testify that although he had visited Calvin's room several times and had called him repeatedly on his cell, Calvin was nowhere to be found. The DA was going to use his testimony to shoot holes all through Calvin's alibi. He hated being put in this position. He didn't want to help the state indict his client, even though they could do that with just the victim's testimony and the DNA results. But more than that, he didn't want to cause Toni any pain. Even though he was convinced that Calvin had raped this girl, the pain that it was causing Toni was unbearable for him to watch.

He wondered why it was so hard for her to see what everybody else saw, why she couldn't see his guilt. *She is obviously in denial.* He hoped that one day, before Calvin was convicted and sentenced, she would finally open her eyes and see him for the monster that he was. Because only a monster could've hurt the young lady in the elevator like that, no matter how much he tried to convince everybody else otherwise.

And when Toni finally came to the realization that her husband was a monster, he would be there for her the same way he'd been there for her for the past two years. Ethan hoped that Toni wouldn't hold his testimony against him.

A few hours later, after testifying in front of the Grand Jury, Calvin and his crew emerged from the courthouse. For the first time since Calvin had been arrested, Joseph was proud of his client and his ability to hold it together. Calvin managed to hold it together and keep his temper in check. He felt he had no other choice—he was fighting for his life.

As they headed down the courthouse stairs towards their awaiting limousine, they noticed that the crowd had nearly doubled in size. Eager reporters rushed them and shoved microphones into their faces and hurled questions at them. "Don't say a word," Joseph advised them as they pushed their way through the mob.

Meanwhile, law enforcement tried to contain the other spectators as protestors and supporters screamed insults at one another. As the scene between the two opposing forces became more heated, blows were thrown and a full-blown fight broke out. People were being thrown, kicked, and beaten. Calvin pulled Toni closer to him to protect her from the violence.

Security quickly ushered them into the limousine, and they managed to escape the scene without injury. Still shaken by the events that had unfolded before them, Toni burst into tears, and Calvin pulled her into his arms to comfort her.

"Is she going to be okay?" Joseph asked. Toni always seemed so strong; he had never seen her fall apart before.

"Yeah, she's going to be fine," Calvin assured him. "She's just a little shaken up right now."

Ethan could only watch in silence as the woman he'd fallen in love with, clung to another man. He wanted to pull her away from Calvin and promise her that it would all be over soon, but he knew that was out of the question. He would just have to wait until Calvin was convicted to be able to console her. *With the Grand Jury testimony now out of the way, it wouldn't be long before Calvin gets indicted and convicted.*

Chapter Seventeen

Weeks later, Joseph was not surprised when the DA informed him that Calvin was indicted by the Grand Jury. What did surprise him was Calvin's reaction to the news.

"So what do we do now?" Calvin asked as they stood out on the lanai by his Olympic-size swimming pool. "How do we get out of this mess?"

"We can talk to the DA and see if they'll take a plea bargain. That could—"

"Plea bargain?" Calvin shook his head. "I can't do a plea bargain. I'm not pleading guilty to a crime I didn't commit."

"Hey, I thought you guys might like something to drink," Toni said. She'd brought out two glasses of ice tea.

"Thanks, Toni." Joseph took a glass.

"Yeah, baby," Calvin said after he took a swallow.

Toni smiled. Ever since Calvin had been indicted for rape and aggravated assault, his whole attitude had changed. He seemed to be shedding his bad-ass image, to reveal the man she fell in love with seven years ago. She attributed this to the indictment, but she didn't care—kindness was kindness, no matter what the reasoning behind it was.

After giving them their drinks, she returned to the house to give them more time to discuss their defense.

"Like I said, I'm not pleading guilty to a crime I didn't commit."

"If you didn't sleep with this girl and you didn't rape her, then how did your semen get inside her? How did you end up on a video assaulting this girl in an elevator? Until we can answer these questions, there is no way I can get you off."

"That's not me in the video."

"It looks like you."

"But it's not—someone's setting me up."

"Who, why, and how?"

"I don't know who, but I know I have made a few enemies since I started rapping."

"You think it's another rapper?"

"I've talked a lot of shit about people. Maybe somebody's trying to pull me down."

"What about the semen?—how in the hell did your semen get on this girl?"

"Who knows? I fuck a lot of women, but I always wear a condom. Maybe someone got a hold of one of them."

"Are you serious? Do you really expect people to believe that?"

"Look, I've got no other way to explain this. Before those detectives showed me those pictures of that girl, I had never seen her."

"Okay . . . say I believe you. Say someone has framed you for this. For someone to go through all this trouble, they must really hate you. Who hates you enough to do all this?"

* * *

"Where are they?" Ethan asked after Toni let him in.

"Out by the pool." Toni studied his face. She could tell he wasn't too happy. "More bad news?"

"Yeah, more lost endorsements and a suit filed by the DJ he hit at the radio station."

"That's all he needs right now—more bad news."

"Toni, Calvin did this to himself. He's tried to hold up this bad-ass persona, and now all his actions have come back to bite him in the ass."

"You think he raped that girl?"

"I *know* he raped her."

"How can you say that? You're his manager; you're supposed to believe in him."

"I'm no fool, Toni. The evidence speaks for itself."

"Then you're saying I'm a fool because I believe him when he say he didn't do this?"

"No, but I'm saying that you are blind if you think he's telling you the truth. You can't say in all honesty that you still believe him."

"I have to believe in him—he's my husband."

"But he's guilty, Toni."

"If you truly believe that, then maybe you should resign as his manager." She crossed her arms.

"When are you going to wake up?"

"He's by the pool with Joseph," was her only response before she walked away.

Ethan found Calvin and Joseph on the lanai.

"What's up?" he said as he approached the men.

"Our client seems to believe that he has been framed, set up."

151

"Set up? By who?"

"That's what we are trying to figure out."

"You can't be serious."

"Why not? I know I didn't rape that girl, but there is so much evidence against me; it's just too convenient."

Ethan shook his head. "I don't believe this."

"Maybe it was you." Calvin suggested.

"What?"

"Maybe *you* set me up. Maybe you're trying to get me out of the way."

"Are you serious?"

"Maybe you're trying to get me out of the way so you can get next to Toni. I see the way you look at her. You're always at her disposal whenever she needs you—you want to get with my wife."

"Okay . . . this is ridiculous. You are trying to blame all this shit on me now. You need help, man . . . seriously."

"C'mon, Calvin," Joseph said, "you know—"

"No, I don't know. This nigga's been creeping around here, peeping at my wife like a dog in heat."

"Look, nigga, if I wanted to get with your wife, I'd get with her. I wouldn't waste my time setting you up for rape. I don't have to get rid of you to get with her. Your stupid ass do enough stupid-ass shit to push your wife away from you. It's just too bad she can't see what an asshole you are!"

"Fuck you, nigga—get the hell outta my house before I get my gun."

"Go ahead and get your gun, you fake-ass wannabe gansta. I'm tired of baby-sitting your silly ass, anyway."

"Ethan—"

"No," Ethan said. "I'm tired of dealing with this silly-ass nigga. This man's married to the most amazing woman in the world, who, for the life of me I can't figure out, has remained by his side even though he has repeatedly taken advantage of her love. He's pocketing millions, got more fans than he could ever dream of, and he goes and throws it all away for a piece of ass." And then to Calvin, "You're one sick and greedy-ass nigga, and this time you went too far. One day, that beautiful woman is going to wake up and leave your sorry ass. One day, she's gonna be gone outta of your life forever, and maybe then and only then will you be able to appreciate what you had."

Hearing the commotion, Toni ran out onto the lanai. "What's going on?"

"Nothing," Ethan said to her. "I was just resigning as his manager." He turned around and looked at Calvin. "By the way, you just lost two more endorsements and you're being sued by that DJ you punched. As your former manager, I thought you should know." He looked back at Toni. "Please wake up," he said to her and then left.

"Calvin, stop him," Toni begged as she stared at her husband.

"Fuck that nigga. He's the reason I'm in this shit now."

Meanwhile, across town at Southern Scope Records, music executives, Tom Drexel, Michael Jeffries, Saundra Pollard, and Steve Winston were gathering to discuss Calvin's future with their company.

Tom started, "As you all know, Calvin Wallace, one of our most promising new talents, has gotten himself into some legal trouble. Got a call from his attorney today informing me that Mr. Wallace has been indicted, and from what his attorney tells me, it doesn't look very good."

"Doesn't look very good?"—Saundra interjected—"That's an understatement. Mr. Wallace will do time for this."

"Yes," Tom said, "that's if the victim follows through with this."

"Is there any indication that she may not?" Michael asked.

"No," Steve answered. "And why would she? He beat the hell out of that girl."

"Allegedly," Tom corrected.

"Yeah right, *allegedly*." Saundra laughed. "You sound like you believe he's innocent."

"It doesn't matter whether I believe he's innocent or not," Tom said. "What we have to decide is whether we are going support him or leave him flapping in the breeze—is he worth the trouble?"

"Well, the boy's talented. In three months, his CD has gone triple platinum. He's sold out concerts all over the country. The people love him," Michael replied.

"Correction—the people used to love him until he got all mixed up in these rape charges. Record sales have fallen fifteen percent since his arrest. Several radio stations have pulled the CD due to pressure from all the feminist groups. Women are mad as hell," Saundra said.

"Listen, Mr. Wallace has what it takes," Tom said, "but all this bad press is bad for business, so we have to decide—Are we going to back him or not?"

"What do we have to do?" Saundra asked.

Tom looked up at his fellow executives. "We suggest to Mr.

Wallace and his attorney that they make the young lady an offer that she can't refuse. She accepts the offer and drops the charges, and we'll honor our contract with him."

"Well," added Michael, "isn't the damage already done by then? I mean it's like Saundra said, 'Women hate him, radio won't play his music.'"

"No," Tom explained. "We live in a very forgiving society. Stars screw up all the time, get a little bad press, and then they're right back on top again. Look at Eddie Murphy—he got arrested for trying to solicit from a transvestite—people still love him; they still go to his movies.

"Kobe Bryant was charged with rape—he gave the girl a little bit of money—people still love him. Then there's Hugh Grant with that prostitute, Snoop Dogg was accused of rape, Bill Cosby, of molestation. People still love them. Hell, Clarence Thomas was accused of sexual harassment, yet they appointed him to the Supreme Court. And then there's the most infamous one of all—R. Kelly. R. Kelly is making music left, right, and center, and he's on video having sex with little girls. Society still loves him. Michael Jackson just beat the charges lodged against him, and the public adores him. Calvin can bounce back too."

"I don't know." Steve scratched his head. "What if he doesn't bounce back? What if society won't forgive him?—then we'll be stuck with this kid that's going nowhere fast."

"Always the pessimist, huh, Steve?" Tom laughed.

"Hey, I'm just trying to keep it real."

"Listen," Tom reminded them. "We're not a huge company. We make a little bit of change here. Calvin Wallace is an investment, and I think we should support him. He's already made millions for our company; besides, you all know that he bust his ass for this company. He's not lazy. I just think he had bad judgment along the way."

"Say we stand by him, what happens if he gets in trouble again?"

Tom took off his wire-rimmed glasses and looked at Steve. "I don't think he'll risk it again; the boy's scared as hell. He's not going to blow it the second time around."

"You really believe in him that much?" Steve asked.

"Yes, and not only do I believe in him, I believe in society's forgiving nature."

Michael added, "But all this is based on whether or not she'll accept the offer; she may not want the money, she may want justice."

"Well," Tom allowed, "if she wants justice and Calvin gets convicted, then there is nothing we can do about that, but we have to a least give her a chance to decide."

Saundra suggested, "I say we give it a try. It couldn't hurt for him to make her an offer."

"Yeah," Michael agreed, "let's see what happens."

Tom looked at Steve. "What do you think?"

"Oh, what the hell . . . it's worth a try."

Tom smiled. "All right, I'll give him a call first thing tomorrow."

The next day Calvin was summoned to Southern Scope Records to meet with Tom Drexel.

"Hey, Calvin," Tom said when entered his office. "Have a seat."

"Mr. Drexel." Calvin sat down on the sofa.

"Tom—call me Tom; we're all family here." Tom walked

over to the mini-bar and prepared himself a drink. "Can I fix you something?" He looked over his shoulder at Calvin.

"I'll take a Hennessy," Calvin answered as he took in the office surroundings.

"Sure thing." Tom fixed the drinks, then walked over and handed Calvin his.

"Thanks."

Tom sat down on the edge of his desk and took a sip of his drink as he studied Calvin. He hoped that he was making the right decision in sticking by this kid, even though he'd gone and messed up his future with this rape nonsense.

Calvin tried to anticipate Tom's reason for summoning him to his office. "Look, I know why I'm here, but sir, you have to believe me when I say that I had nothing to do with what happened to that girl. I—"

"Calvin, Calvin, Calvin . . . calm down and relax. You don't have to convince me that you're innocent—I don't care. Hell, Southern Scope Records doesn't give a damn whether you're guilty or not. We hope you're innocent, but we don't give a damn if you're not."

"Then why am I here?"

"We want you to make it go away." Tom smiled and took a sip of his drink.

"Make it go away?"

"Yes—make the rape and assault charges go away."

"And how am I supposed to do that?—kill her?"

Tom chuckled. "You're funny, Calvin—of course not. Then we'd have a murder on our hands. What we want you to do is to offer her some money, a settlement, if you will."

"Pay her off?"

"Exactly."

157

"But I didn't rape her."

"Now, now, Calvin, it doesn't matter whether you raped her or not. Kobe said he didn't rape that girl in Colorado, but he offered her a settlement."

"Yeah, but the rape charges were already dropped; she was suing him."

"A payoff is a payoff, don't get it twisted."

"If I pay her off, then won't people think I'm guilty?"

"They already think you're guilty, so what's the problem?"

Calvin thought about Tom's suggestion.

"Look Calvin, it's a no-brainer. Southern Scope Records wants to support you. We believe in your ability to put asses in the seats and bills in the registers, but as long as these charges are hanging over your head, record sales will continue to drop, radio stations will not start playing your songs again, and you're gonna do time for this. If you offer this girl some money and she accepts it, drops the charges, you can get back to doing what you do—making music, touring, performing at sold-out shows. This is what you've dreamed about all your life. Don't let some chick stand in the way of that."

Calvin nodded his head.

"And you've got that pretty little wife. You don't want to leave her out here by herself while you're doing fifteen to twenty in the state pen. Soon as the brothas know that you're locked up, they're gonna swoop down on her like vultures on a jack rabbit."

Calvin thought about Toni. He thought about his career. If he couldn't get the girl to drop the rape charges against him, he knew he would lose it all. There were thousands of eager and gifted rappers waiting to take his place at Southern Scope Records and even more men waiting to get their chance at Toni. He knew he treated her like shit, but he loved her and wasn't ready to lose her because of this nonsense. Then he thought about Ethan. He imagined him all packed and ready to move in on Toni just as soon as they locked the prison doors. *Hell no, muthafucka—you'll never have Toni.*

"So what do you say, my man? Make the girl an offer, and we will stand behind you."

"I'll give it a try." It was his only chance of holding on to his freedom, his career, and his wife.

Toni opened the door to her home to find her three closest friends, Jamise Taylor, Karen Mosley, and Shanté Adams, standing outside.

Her mouth dropped open. "What the hell are y'all crazy bitches doing here?" She laughed.

"Divine intervention," the three girls sang out in unison as they all began to hug her.

When they released her, she ushered them into the house.

"Humph," Shanté said as Toni led them through the huge foyer and into the living room. "It's no wonder you don't come down to the hood no more . . . you living like this."

"I don't come down to the hood no more 'cause I ain't been invited."

Karen chuckled as she surveyed her surroundings. "Never knew you had to be invited to come back home. Impressive." She looked back at Toni. "Girl, you are living it up."

"Thanks, girl. You would've seen my place sooner, had you accepted all the invitations I extended to y'all."

"Some of us have to work," Jamise teased, "we didn't marry rich rap stars."

159

"Yeah, yeah, yeah. Why don't y'all let me give you a tour of my place?"

"Very tempting. But we didn't come to get a tour of your place, we came to check up on you. How you doing, girl?" Karen asked in a sincere tone.

Toni smiled. "I'm doing fine."

"We know about Calvin and the rape."

"It's a mistake."

"You can't be serious. What kind of bullshit is he feeding you?"

"Listen, Calvin didn't rape that girl. He's never seen her before."

"Then how in the hell did his cum get all over her?"

"I don't know." Toni shook her head. "He thinks he was set up."

Shanté laughed. "So that's the bullshit he's been feeding her."

"Don't you know what he did to that girl? He beat the hell out of her, fucked her, and then left her in the elevator."

"Calvin didn't do that, I'm telling you."

The look of frustration was all over her friends' faces as they tried to figure how she could be so blind.

"How can you say that?" Jamise asked. "With all the evidence that they have against him, he can't be innocent. And you can't honestly tell us that you think he is."

"He's my husband; I have to believe him. I can't abandon him. What kind of wife would I be if I just took off 'cause things got a little hot?"

"A little hot? Toni, it's a towering inferno up in here. That man hasn't treated you right since he got that record deal. He's been fuckin' all over town and doesn't even have the decency to hide it from you or your family or your friends. He's a fuckin' asshole, and how you still sleep with him is beyond me. I'm surprised he hasn't infected you with something yet. And thank God, you haven't gotten pregnant by him."

"Toni," Shanté added, "the man's been charged with rape. You know he can't keep his dick in his pants. You need to leave that sick son of a bitch."

"Honey, I'm home," Calvin sang out as he strolled into the living room.

Toni jumped. "Calvin, I didn't expect you back so soon." She stood up and silently prayed that he hadn't heard any of their conversation.

But Calvin had heard plenty of the conversation. Enough to know that her friends were trying to talk her into leaving him. "Things went a little bit quicker than expected, but it's all good." He walked over to her and slipped one of his arms around her waist as he looked at her friends. "Jamise, Shanté, Karen," he said acknowledging them, "glad you finally made it by to see Toni. She misses you all a lot."

Jamise stood up and crossed her arms. "We miss her too, Calvin."

"So," he said looking down at Toni and then back at her friends, "what's the special occasion? Is someone getting married, pregnant?" He knew all too well why they'd shown up after all this time.

"We just come to check on our friend," Karen told him.

"Hmmm . . . that's funny. In all the time that we've been

living here, y'all haven't come by to check on your best friend. Something must be going on for you to travel all this way."

"Calvin—"

"No, Toni." Shanté stood up and put one hand on her hip. She stared at Calvin. "To tell the truth, Calvin, we come to rescue our girl."

He laughed. "Rescue your girl?" He glanced down at Toni and tightened his grip around her waist. He looked back at Shanté. "From what?"

"From you."

"Me?—what the hell did I do?"

"You're a fuckin' idiot." Shanté didn't blink.

"Shanté," Toni said.

"Nah, nah, baby, I got this." Calvin pulled his arm away from Toni's waist and walked up to her.

Karen quickly rose to her feet, and the three girls stood there facing him as a united front.

"You don't know me, Shanté. Why would you say something so crude about somebody you don't even know?"

"I know you, Calvin. We all know you. You may have been straight with Toni back in high school, but we know that since you've become this big-ass rapper you've been treating our girl like sh—"

"Shanté—" Toni tried to interrupt.

"Toni, no. We got this." Jamise held her hand up for her to stop. "Your nigga needs to hear this." She kept her eyes focused on Calvin and the cocky grin he had on his face. "You've got this beautiful woman here who loves the hell out of you. Niggas been trying to get with her since day one, but

162

she wasn't hearing it. She loves Calvin. She believes in Calvin. She's sticking with Calvin. She sacrificed everything to be with you. She let go of college because she was too busy trying to support you and your fuckin' dreams."

The attack upset Calvin. "My fuckin' dreams? My fuckin' dreams are what put her in the phat-ass mansion. My fuckin' dreams are why she's flossing Dolce & Gabbana and Gucci and Donna Karan. My fuckin' dreams are why she's dining at the finest, upscale restaurants in town and why she's rolling around here in that pimped-out Jaguar, and why I have Jacob the jeweler on speed dial. That's what standing by me and my fuckin' dreams have gotten her." Jamise took a step toward him and pushed her finger in his face. "Yeah . . . and your fuckin' dreams is why she's at home every night in this phat-ass mansion, with her Cristal, and 400 count sheets, crying all alone while you're out fuckin' some whore who wouldn't, if you were dying of thirst, wouldn't waste her spit on you, if you didn't have a recognizable face and phat-ass pockets.

"You see, Toni was here when you didn't have a pot to piss in or a window to throw it out, and you can't find twenty minutes to give to her because you are too busy running around here, shoving your dick down every open mouth you can find."

"Then open a little wider, bitch, so I can let you have a suck."

Before he knew what happened, Calvin felt the burning sting of Jamise's hand across the face.

"No!" Toni screamed. She grabbed Calvin and pulled him back away from her friend.

"Don't worry, Toni." Calvin laughed and rubbed his cheek. "It didn't hurt; she hits like a girl."

"You arrogant son of a bitch!" Jamise yelled.

"You bitches get the hell out of my house," Calvin said, casually dismissing them.

"Fuck you, nigga!"

"That's it, isn't it? You're just mad 'cause I never wanted to fuck you broke-down ho's."

Karen ignored his remark. "Toni . . . leave him, Toni—he's a rapist and a whore."

"Get the fuck outta my house!" he yelled before Toni could respond.

"Toni, please . . . you can do so much better than this; you deserve better than this."

"Just go," she begged as she shook her head.

"Toni . . ."

"You heard her, bitch—now get the hell outta my house before I call the police!"

The girls looked at their friend.

She shook her head no again as her eyes pleaded for them to leave.

Calvin pulled out his cell phone.

"Calvin, no." Toni pushed the phone down. "They're leaving." She looked over at them.

Jamise pulled Toni to her and hugged her. "You give us a call if you need anything."

"I will." Toni nodded then hugged the other two girls before they left.

Once the girls were out the door, Calvin took Toni by her upper arm and turned her to him. "Are you trying to leave me?" He looked down at her.

"No." She stared up at him, expecting to find anger and frustration; instead, she found confusion. "Baby, I love you. I would never leave you."

"Toni, I need you more than ever right now. Your friends are right—you have always been down for me, no matter what. Even when I was an ass, you stayed right by my side and believed in me even when I didn't believe in myself. I need you to believe in me now. I need you to believe that I didn't rape that girl; that someone's set me up."

"Who? Who would do this to you?"

"I don't know. Ethan is the only person I can come up with."

"Why would he do something like this?"

"It doesn't matter. What matters to me right now is that I have you in my corner . . . do I?"

Toni was on the verge of tears. "Of course."

"From this moment on, I'm going to stop taking you for granted. I'm going to stop whorin' around and treat you like you're supposed to be treated, do you hear me?"

"Yes."

"You want a baby?"

"What?"

"You talked about us having a baby a while back."

"But Calvin—"

"I want a baby. I want one with you. I want us to be a family." He slipped his finger under her chin and tilted her face toward him as he lowered his lips on top of hers. He kissed her slowly, gently. He kissed her in a way that he hadn't kissed her in years.

But she remembered. It was the kind of kiss that was laced

with the love that he promised her over three years ago when he said, "I do."

He pulled her closer, his hands molding the soft curves of her body to his.

She could feel his hardness straining against her belly as she pressed her body even closer to his.

Slowly Calvin pulled his lips away from hers only to press them against her ear. "I want to make love to my wife."

Toni nodded.

He slipped his hands down to her hips and lifted her up, wrapping her legs around his waist. Then he carried her up the spiral staircase to their bedroom. Gently, he laid her down on the bed and peeled her clothes away until she lay naked before him.

Toni watched as he removed his own clothes and then joined her on the bed.

He gathered her into his arms as he kissed her lips, her neck, her fingertips, and her soul.

Toni's hands moved over the smooth, chocolate skin of his chest, thighs, and back as she urged him to take her.

But he wouldn't rush. He was going to take his time and make love to her all night long like he should have been doing for the past three years of their marriage. He pushed her legs apart, revealing the warmth entrance of her womanhood that had brought him so much pleasure so many nights. Now it was his turn to return the favor. He kissed the full lips of her vagina and then gently pushed them apart to gain access to her swollen clitoris that was aching to be kissed. Tenderly he teased her and taunted her with his lips and tongue as she moved her hips up to meet every stroke.

She moaned and wriggled beneath his mouth as he

brought her more pleasure than she'd ever dreamed possible. And when she could take no more, she screamed out his name and climaxed. As her body shivered against his hungry mouth, he lapped up her juices, not wanting to miss a drop.

Slowly, her body began to recover and relax again.

It was then that Calvin raised his head up and positioned himself between her legs.

She stared up at him as he hovered over her.

"Let's make a baby." He guided himself inside her.

She gasped when his hardness filled her up. She wrapped her legs around his waist as he drove himself deeper inside her.

As their passion rose, so did their rhythm. Each stroke went deeper than the previous one, and she met each one with such intensity, he knew she was going to cum again.

"Come on, baby," he whispered in her ear. "Come on and give it to me."

"Oh, Calvin," she cried out as she reached ecstasy again. Seconds later, he joined her as he gripped her tight, called out her name, and spilled his juices inside her.

As they lay there recovering from their lovemaking, Calvin raised his head and looked down at his wife. For the first time in years, he wanted to hold on to her all night. Reluctantly, he rolled off of her. He pulled her into his arms and promised her that it was going to be like that from that moment on—he was going to be the man she needed him to be.

Chapter Eighteen

A few weeks later, Ethan anxiously waited for Toni in a nearby hotel room. He paced the floor as he tried to think of what to say to her.

He was practicing. "Toni. Hello, Toni. Toni you look beautiful." He let out a deep sigh. Catching a glimpse of himself in a mirror, he stopped pacing and stared at himself. "What are you doing?" he said to himself. "Toni's a married woman. You're in love with a married woman." He shook his head. *This is wrong.* He wondered if he had time enough to call her and tell her not to meet her. As he glanced at his watch, he heard a knock at the door. "Too late," he said to himself.

"Toni," he said when he opened the door. She was even more beautiful than he remembered, but he fought the urge to tell her that. "I'm glad you came." He stepped back so she could enter.

"I'm glad that you called." She looked around the room and then up at him after he closed the door. "I hated the way things ended for you and Calvin. I wanted to see you, to see how you were doing."

"I'm good." He forced a nervous smile. "How are you?"

"I'm good too." She smiled back. "I miss seeing you, having you around."

"I miss being around, to tell you the truth." He took a deep breath to calm his nerves. "How's Calvin doing?" He wanted to get all of the niceties out of the way before he told her why he asked her to meet him there.

"He's doing well." She was excited to tell him. "He made a settlement with the DJ for a few dollars, and Joseph is arranging for him to meet with Tamela Waters and her lawyer. They want to offer a settlement if she drops the charges against him."

"So things are going to work out for him, after all?"

"Yes." Her mood changed to a more somber one. "Calvin swears that you set him up. He's telling anybody that will listen that you framed him."

"You believe him?"

"I don't know what to believe. I just know that he didn't rape that girl."

"So you think *I* did it? You think I set him up? Please tell me you don't believe that, Toni—you know me better than that."

"I told you I don't know what to believe. I just—"

Ethan shook his head and walked away from her. He stopped and turned around to face her again. "I can't believe he's got you believing that bullshit."

"I said I—"

"Can't you see that he's just trying to cover his ass? How can you still believe him after knowing about all the evidence they have against him? How can you even think I would do something like that?"

"I'm sorry." She could see he was genuinely hurt by the accusation. "It's just that it's all I have left."

"It's so easy to believe that I could set him up, but you can't believe that your husband, who's treated you like shit, fucked around on you repeatedly, doesn't have it in him to rape someone?"

"I have to believe in him."

"Why, Toni? Why are you so hell-bent on believing he's so innocent?"

"I have to."

"Why?"

"Because, it's what I need to believe to stand by his side throughout all this."

"Why do you have to stand by him? He's treated you like shit, totally disrespected you."

"If I stand by him through all this, then maybe he'll see that I am all that he needs. Maybe he'll see that I'll always be there for him, and he'll leave all those other women alone."

"You really believe he has it in him to see the value in you? You really think he'll stop fuckin' around on you if you stand by him?"

"He's changing, Ethan. Maybe you don't see it. Maybe the whole damn world doesn't see it, but I do. Soon we're going to be a family again. He says he's through with those other girls; that he's going to be there for me."

"And how many times has he promised to stop chasing after those other women? How many times has he promised to be faithful to you?"

"It's real this time . . . I can feel it. He means it this time. I can see he's starting to appreciate mc now."

"Do you think he'll ever be able to appreciate you, Toni? Really appreciate you the way I do?"

She stared at him. "What do you mean, 'the way you do?'"

He walked over to her and looked down at her. "Calvin was right about one thing—I do care about you, Toni. I care about you a lot more than I should."

She didn't say anything; she didn't know what to say.

"You are a good woman and you deserve a good man. Now, I may not have the kind of money that your husband has and I may not be able to put you up in a six-million-dollar home, but I can love you in a way that he will never know how." He stepped closer.

Her lips parted to speak, but no words came out.

Before he could stop himself, he pulled her into his arms and covered her mouth with his.

Instead of pulling away like she knew she should have, she kissed him back as her arms went up and around his neck. Their bodies molded together as one, as they submitted to the feelings that had grown between them throughout the past couple of years.

Ethan thought he was dreaming as he held her small frame in his arms and savored the sweetness of her soft lips. *It couldn't be a dream*, he thought to himself, because never in his dream would she taste like this. He slipped his hands down her waist to her hips and picked her up, wrapped her lags around his waist and carried over to the bed. Slowly, he lowered her down on the bed as he lay down on top of her.

Toni felt a stirring inside her, an aching to have him. She moaned as his lips abandoned her mouth and made their way down to her neck.

His tongue tasted the sweetness of her flesh as he pushed

his hips against her, forcing her to feel his erect penis. His throbbing manhood strained to free itself from the restriction of his pants. He wanted to be inside her, to make love to her over and over again. His lips traveled down to her breasts. The thin fabric of her blouse prevented him from having full access to her breasts, but he managed to capture one in his mouth and began to nurse, his hand massaging the other.

Suddenly feeling guilty, Toni whispered, "Ethan . . . we can't do this."

He raised his head up and looked down into her eyes. "I love you, Toni. I love you and I want to be with you."

She stared up at him. Half of her wanted to surrender to what she was feeling inside, but the other half knew it wasn't right.

"Calvin doesn't deserve you; he doesn't know how to love you."

"I can't," she finally managed to say. She gently pushed him off her, and he let her up. As she sat up on the edge of the bed, she nervously straightened her clothes.

Ethan knelt down in front of her and took her hand. "Baby—"

"No." She pulled her hand away and stood up. "Don't do this to me." She started to cry softly. "Don't ask me to leave my husband." She hurried towards the door, trying to avoid his eyes.

"Toni"—He grabbed her upper arm and turned her around to face him—"I know you care about me; I can feel it in your kiss, I see it in your eyes. You love me, don't you?"

"Ethan, why are you doing this?" Toni looked up at him, tears streaming down her face.

"Because I love you. You do love me, don't you?" He searched her eyes for an answer.

She quickly turned her head and pulled away from him. "I can't do this to Calvin." She turned and hurried to the door.

Ethan followed. When she grabbed the knob and pulled the door open, he quickly pushed it shut and pressed his body against the back of hers. He lowered his lips to her ears. "I love you, Toni. Please don't leave me here like this."

She could feel his warm breath against her skin. Without turning around, she responded with, "I'm sorry. I just can't do this. Not right now. Not when he needs me the most." She pulled the door open and left.

Ethan watched as Toni hurried down the hallway. *How in the hell did he do it? How in the hell did Calvin rape a woman, possibly avoid going to jail by paying her off and at the same time keep his beautiful wife right by his side the entire time supporting him?* He couldn't explain it.

After watching Toni step inside the elevator, he stepped back inside the hotel room to gather his wits.

What was he expecting? Did he really expect her to drop everything, announce that she was in love with him too, and run off with him? He didn't know, but at least she knew how he felt. His feelings were no longer a secret. He wondered, *Would she tell Calvin about their meeting or would she keep it to herself?*

As Toni hurried through the hotel lobby and across the parking lot to her car, she kept telling herself not to look back. She was afraid he might be following her because, if he was, she might turn around and run back into his arms. Silently she prayed that he'd stayed in the room.

It was only after she made it to the safety of her car that

she dared to look back. Both a wave of relief and disappointment washed over her when she realized that he wasn't pursuing her. She looked back at the hotel and thought about his lips against hers, about his hands on her body, about the heat between them.

Although she always had a small crush on Ethan, she never knew he had feelings for her. *He had been so careful to not reveal what he was feeling inside, until now. Now that he was no longer working for Calvin, he must have felt it was okay to let me know how he felt, but it wasn't okay.* She was still married to Calvin; he was still her husband, no matter how he'd treated her, no matter what he did or didn't do. She had to stand by him, had to support him. And no matter what her feelings for Ethan were, she couldn't leave Calvin.

Chapter Nineteen

A few weeks later, Calvin and Joseph arrived at the Gaithers, Stellars, and Wall law firm to discuss the settlement they were going to offer Tamela Waters. Although Calvin wasn't too excited about making his accuser an offer, the thought of losing everything was enough to make him go through with the plan. And with all the evidence the police had gathered against him, he knew no jury would acquit him.

"Listen, Calvin," Joseph said as they took their seats in the conference room and waited for Tamela and her lawyer, "let me handle everything. You sit back and remain cool, and I'll make this happen. You know how hot-headed you are. We don't want to blow this. If you lose it in here, then you might as well kiss your freedom goodbye for the next fifteen to twenty years, do you understand?"

"Yeah, man. Just do your magic and make this shit go away."

Soon after, Lisa Stellars, Tamela's attorney, entered the

conference room. "Good day, gentlemen." Lisa placed her briefcase on the table and extended her hand to Joseph. "I'm Lisa Stellars, counsel for Miss Waters."

Joseph quickly rose to his feet and shook her hand. "Joseph Raymond, counsel for Mr. Wallace."

Calvin sat up when he noticed that his accuser wasn't present. "Where is she? Where the hell is this girl?"

"I'm sorry, but Miss Waters decided not to attend this meeting today. She was too afraid to see Mr. Wallace again and understandably so." Lisa took her seat.

"What the hell are you talking about, 'understandably so?' I didn't do shit to that girl. I never laid a hand on her and she's afraid of me?"

"Calvin, calm down," Joseph warned.

"Hell no! This girl accused me of rape and then is too scared to show her face. I want to see her. I want to see my accuser."

"Mr. Wallace," Lisa said, "it is very easy to see that you have an uncontrollable temper and my client has already been the recipient of your wrath—"

"Listen here, bitch," Calvin said, rising to his feet, "I'll show you my wrath!"

"Calvin, don't blow this." Calvin shook his head in disbelief. "I can't believe this shit."

"Mr. Raymond," Lisa said as she stood up, "if you cannot calm your client down, then you'll force me to end these proceedings and inform Miss Waters that we will be going to trial."

"Just a second," he said to Lisa. Then to Calvin, "Let me

talk to you for a minute." He took him by the arm and led him away from the table, out of Lisa's earshot.

"What, man? You know this is some bogus bullshit. Here I'm supposed to offer this chick some money and she don't even show up."

"Calvin, her lawyer's here. That is all we need to make this go away."

"But I want to see her—I don't give a damn about her fuckin' lawyer."

"Why? Why do you want to see her?"

"Because I want to look into the eyes of the woman that accused me of rape. I want to look into the woman's eyes that fucked up my life."

"Well, here's news for you, Calvin—it's not going to happen, not today, so get over it."

"Get over it? This shit's not happening to you; this girl is ruining my life."

"And that's exactly why we're here. We're gonna put and end to this, but I need your help, Calvin. I need you to cooperate. Southern Scope is behind you, your wife is behind you, but I can't do anything for you unless you cooperate."

He breathed out in frustration. "Yeah, I hear you."

"Then let me do my job, okay?"

"Just get me the fuck outta here."

"Will do." He slapped Calvin on the back, and they walked back over to the table, where Lisa was still patiently waiting for them.

"Sorry about that, Ms. Stellars. You can understand that my client is a little upset, but we both want to get this over and done with ASAP."

"No problem." Lisa forced a smile. "I'll try to make this as painless as possible."

"Thank you."

Joseph and Calvin sat back down.

Lisa opened her briefcase and pulled some papers out. "I assure you that Miss Waters has given me complete authority with respect to this settlement with your client, so this can be over as soon as possible, as long we all keep an open mind."

"So what kind of numbers are we talking about?" Joseph asked.

"Well, after discussing this extensively with my client, we've come up with a number that we think is more than fair. We've included hospital bills, pain and suffering, counseling that she will need to get over this traumatic experience—"

"What's the number?" Joseph asked impatiently.

"We think that twenty-five million is more than fair." Lisa pulled out a folder and slid it over to Joseph.

Just as Joseph reached for the folder, Calvin blurted out, "Twenty-five million?—Hell no!" and shoved the folder back toward Lisa. "You bitches must be outta your fuckin' minds!"

"Calvin, let me handle this." Joseph turned to Lisa. "I'm sorry, Ms. Stellars. We're just so surprised by such a high dollar amount. Miss Waters can't seriously expect my client to pay her twenty-five million dollars."

"My client was hospitalized for over a week. She has suffered greatly mentally and emotionally from the assault— her life will never be the same."

"But twenty-five million?"

"That's chump change for your client. He already has a

substantial amount of income and the potential to make millions more; he can afford twenty-five million."

"But he doesn't have twenty-five million dollars."

"No, but his record company does. That is why we are here, right? They want to make this go away."

"Still . . . we can't do twenty-five."

"Can your client do fifteen to twenty in the state penitentiary? I don't know that any jury will find your client not guilty of rape. And a rapper behind bars doesn't make as much money as one out on the road. So, tell me, how bad does Southern Scope Records want to see Mr. Wallace out there making money?"

"This is fuckin' extortion." Calvin stood up and walked over to the window. He wasn't sure how much more of this he could take.

Joseph ignored the outburst. "I've been authorized to go as high as ten million,"

"Ten million?" Lisa shook her head. "That's not quite what we are looking for; I believe you can do better than that."

"How much better?"

"Fifteen million."

"Fifteen million?" Joseph looked over at Calvin and then back at Lisa. "Could you give me a minute? I need to make a phone call."

"Sure." Lisa stood up, gathered her papers, and left the room.

Joseph stood up and pulled out his cell phone. He walked over to where Calvin was standing by the window and put his hand on his shoulder. "You all right, man?"

"Twenty-five million? Hell no! Fifteen million? Hell no!

Give that bitch fifty cents and tell her not spend it all in one place."

"Southern Scope Records is footing the bill for this, remember?"

"Yeah, but my black ass have to work off all that fuckin' loot."

"At least you'll be a free man."

"Yeah, whatever."

Joseph dialed the number to Southern Scope Records. "Hello, may I speak with Tom Drexel please."

"Who may I say is calling?" the receptionist asked.

"Joseph Raymond."

"Just a moment, Mr. Raymond."

A few seconds later, Tom was on the phone. "So how is it going?"

"Not bad. They want fifteen million."

"Fifteen million?" Tom repeated. "Greedy, aren't they?"

"Yes, sir, they are."

Tom exhaled loudly. "Well, give them the fifteen million and get them out of our hair."

"Yes, sir." Joseph watched Calvin fuming still. After hanging up his cell, he placed a hand on Calvin's shoulder. "It's almost over."

Calvin looked at him. "How in the hell did this happen? How in the hell did I end up here buying my freedom for fifteen million dollars because of a crime I didn't commit? How in the hell in America can shit like this happen?"

"You're one of the lucky ones. You're lucky you can afford to do this; most people can't."

After summoning Lisa back to the conference room, they all sat back down at the table.

"So what do you have for me? Is your client's freedom worth fifteen million dollars to Southern Scope Records?" Lisa asked.

"Yes, it is. We are prepared to pay Miss Waters fifteen million dollars to drop the charges."

"Good. Now let's get the paperwork done."

Chapter Twenty

A couple of weeks later, Toni nervously paced the floor of their den as she waited for a call. Calvin left for Southern Scope Records a few hours earlier to meet with executives to discuss their strategy for repairing his damaged reputation. Tamela had dropped all charges against him, but he was still bitter about having to give her a settlement to make it all go away. And even though his record company had paid the settlement to Tamela, it was considered an advance to Calvin—so it still came out of his pocket.

The phone rang. Toni stopped pacing and stared at it. She knew it was the call she was waiting for. She wanted to run over and answer it, but her nerves had her frozen. There was no turning back now. All her hard work had led to this moment.

The phone rang for a third time. She took a deep breath, let it out, and walked over to it. She picked up the receiver. "Hello."

After the call, she walked over to her computer, made a few keystrokes, and then stared at the screen. Seconds later, she saw what she wanted to see. Slowly, a smile formed on her lips. It was done. *Finally.* "It actually worked," she said to herself. Thank God for criminal investigative TV shows like "Law and Order," "CSI," "City Confidential," and "Cold Case Files." All those nights she spent sitting alone drinking up information from these shows while her husband was out fucking complete strangers gave her the tools she needed to carry out her plan.

She picked up the phone and called a few people to tell them everything was a go.

After hanging up the phone, she thought about Calvin. She wondered how things were going at the record company, and what his reaction would be once he found out what she'd done. *Should I leave him a letter or tell him in person? Or maybe I shouldn't tell him at all. Maybe I should let him find out for himself when he returned home.* He'd find all of her personal effects gone, and then he'd know that she'd left him. She wondered if leaving him like that would make her seem cruel and uncaring. She smiled to herself. *It would be no crueler than what I'd already done to him.*

Toni reached into her purse and pulled out a set of keys—keys to her new apartment. Her apartment was tiny compared to the mansion she was leaving behind. But the 2,400-square-foot apartment would suit her new single lifestyle very well. She slipped the keys back into her purse, sat down in her husband's favorite recliner, and waited for her movers to arrive.

Fifteen minutes later, they were there. She instructed the men on what items to take and what to leave. Although she didn't have much—mainly clothes—the guys had plenty to do, in terms of boxing up her items and loading them onto the truck. As they packed up her belongings, she casually strolled around her soon-to-be former home for one last look at what she was leaving behind.

As Calvin turned his Navigator down the street that he lived, he thought about the meeting with the executives at Southern Scope Records. As they discussed ways of cleaning up his reputation and getting him back into the hearts of his fans, all he could think about was Toni. She'd been his rock.

Although the record company paid off Tamela, they didn't believe he was innocent. Joseph was by his side during the majority of what he now called the "Rape Crisis," only because he was paid to be. Ethan, whom he was sure mastermined the whole thing to get next to Toni, had disappeared.

But Toni was there for him, when no one else believed in him. When her friends and family tried to tell her to jump ship, she remained steadfast and by his side. Even when he did the unspeakable and forced himself on her, Toni didn't flinch. She made it crystal clear that she believed in him and that she was always going to be there.

Not only had he taken her love for granted, but he had taken advantage of it as well. But things had changed. Nearly losing his freedom, his career, and his wife had put everything in a different perspective for him. Toni was a queen. She was his queen, and from this point on, he was going to treat her as such. No more giving her loving to strangers, no more disrespecting her, he was going to make sure she had everything she wanted, whenever she wanted; the way she wanted. He was going to take care of her.

As Calvin pulled up to his home, he noticed a moving

truck parked out front and guys loading boxes into the back of it.

"What the hell . . ." He parked and jumped out of his car. "Yo, man, what the hell is going on?" he asked as he approached one of the movers.

"Just following orders, man," the mover said as he loaded the box onto the truck.

"Whose orders? Whose shit is this?"

"Don't ask me, ask him." The mover pointed at another guy loading boxes onto the back of the truck.

"What's the problem?" the other man asked when he noticed Calvin.

"Who told you to move this shit?"

"And who are you?"

"I'm the owner of this fuckin' house."

"Yo, man, just calm down; we're just doing our job."

"Who told you to move this?"

"Let's see," he said as he walked over to the cab of the truck, opened the door, and retrieved the info from the front seat. He read the name off the papers—"A Toni Wallace," the guy said and then handed the papers to Calvin.

Without even looking at the papers, Calvin turned and rushed up the stairs and into the house. "Toni," he called out as he searched for her. After searching unsuccessfully for his wife downstairs, Calvin raced up the spiral staircase, taking them two at a time. "Toni, where the hell are you?"

Toni turned around and looked up at Calvin as he entered their bedroom. "Calvin," she said, "I didn't expect you back so soon."

"Obviously." He walked up to her and stared down at her

in bewilderment. "What the hell is going on? Are you leaving me?"

"Yes." She turned to walk away.

Calvin grabbed her upper arm and turned her back around to face him. "What? But why?" He stumbled over his words. "Why are you leaving me? All the rape charges have been dropped; things are just getting back to normal."

"That's the problem, Calvin—things are going to go back to normal. For the past three years, you have treated me like shit. You have fucked around on me without the decency to hide it from me."

"But, baby, that's all changed. I've changed. I'm through with all those other girls. It's just you and me now, baby; it's us against the world."

"No." She shook her head. "I can't believe you, Calvin."

"Baby, I promise . . . all my running around is over."

"You promised me that two years ago, but you never stopped; you just got worse. You just found more women to cheat with."

"I was stupid back then, Toni. I didn't know what I had; now I do. I really mean it this time, baby. Almost going to jail, losing my freedom, my career, almost losing you has changed my whole outlook. Things are different now. We can start a family like you always wanted. We can have a whole bunch of babies, go to school plays, PTA meetings, soccer games, the whole nine yards. Anything you want, Toni. Everything you want. It's yours."

"It's too late; I've made up my mind."

"Toni, you can't leave me, baby. I need you. You're all I've got left."

"I'm sorry, Calvin. You've hurt me one too many times." Toni pulled her arm away from him and walked toward the bedroom door.

"You really leaving me? After all the shit we've been through, you're leaving me now?"

She didn't answer as she walked out of the door.

Realizing he was losing the battle, Calvin decided he couldn't go down like a punk, begging a woman to stay with him. He was Blayze. Women begged him to stay with them, not the other way around. *What in the hell am I doing?* Out of both anger and hurt, he yelled out after Toni. "Then fuck you, bitch; I was through with you anyway!"

Toni stopped just above the staircase, turned around, and walked back into the bedroom. "What did you just say?"

"I said 'fuck you.'"

"Fuck *me?*"

"Yeah, fuck you, *Antoinette Michelle Wallace.* Fuck you *and* the horse you rode in on."

"No, you're the one who just got fucked."

"No, you're fucked because you're leaving here with nothing. You signed that prenuptial agreement, so you don't get a damn thing from me. All that ice that you're used to rocking, all those famous labels that you're used to wearing on your back, all that shit is gone. So you can take your sorry ass down to Wal-Mart and get a job application to pay your new fuckin' bills . . . 'cause you ain't getting shit from me."

"Ha!" she laughed. "That fuckin' prenup—that was always your ace in the hole, the one thing you constantly held over my head to keep me from leaving—fuck that little piece of paper that I signed when I was too dumb to know any better. And guess what, Calvin—you just got fucked by me. I just fucked you long and hard with a ten-inch dick right up your pretty little black ass and you didn't even know it."

"What the hell are you talking about?"

"I didn't want to tell you this, but since you asked so nicely, I'll answer your questions. But first I have a few for you. And, by the way, you may want to sit down for this 'cause this shit just might knock you down on that pretty little black ass that you're always bragging about." She smiled. Suddenly she got a warm and fuzzy feeling about her impending confession. Her dear husband was about to get the shock of his life.

Instead of sitting down like his wife suggested, Calvin just crossed his arms as he prepared for her revelation. *This is going to be good.*

"Suit yourself," she said, noting his stubbornness. Then she started, "Did you ever wonder why I believed you when you said you didn't rape that girl? When all the evidence came back and pointed towards you, when your family and friends turned their backs on you and said you were guilty, you ever wonder why I stood by your side?"

Calvin did wonder, but he just assumed that she knew him well enough to know he could never do anything like that, never mind forcing himself on her.

"I believed you because I know you didn't rape that girl. I know this because I know she was never raped."

"What?"

"Tamela was never raped. Everything that happened to her on that faithful night, she welcomed."

"What the hell are you talking about, Toni? I saw pictures of that girl, and the whole thing was caught on video. Somebody raped her. Somebody beat the hell out of her and raped her."

191

"No, Calvin, I'm sorry to disappoint you, but nobody raped that girl. You see, she was acting, and so was the man who attacked her. I hired both her and your impersonator."

"What?"

"When you accused Ethan of setting you up, you were half right; you were set up—but not by Ethan. Ethan would never do anything like that; he's too much of a nice guy. Hell! He still thinks you're guilty. No, *I* was the one that set you up for the rape."

"Toni, why?" He was baffled. Why in the world would his wife set him up for rape? "No," he said to himself, "she didn't do this. She's just lying to hurt me."

"No, no." She shook her index finger at him as if he were a child. "Before we get to the why, we're going to do this like they do on the soap operas—I'm going to tell you how." She put her finger away and then strolled across the floor to the window as she thought about what to say next.

When she was ready, she turned around and looked at him. "Remember that morning before you left to go on tour, when I sucked your dick and you came in my mouth? Didn't you think it was odd that after the way you treated me the night before that I would reward you with a blowjob? Well, there was a reason behind my actions—I needed your sperm and that was the only way I could get it. You see," she said as she crossed her arms, "I didn't spit your cum in the toilet like I normally do. That morning, I saved it."

"What—"

"No interruptions." Then she continued, "I gave it to a young lady by the name of Tamela Waters. You remember her, don't you? Well, of course you've never met her, but she knows exactly who you are. But I digress . . ."

"Tamela," he said to himself. *Did Toni really know her? Did she really give her my semen?* He wasn't convinced; her story was too incredible.

"Anyway, after you got to your hotel room, you received a celebratory bottle of Cristal from me. That bottle of Cristal had been drugged with 'roofies,' you know, the 'date rape' drug. Although roofies normally come in pill or powdered form, I was able to find it in liquid form and I added it to the bottle of Cristal, using a syringe. I gave that to Tamela too. She was here in Atlanta and after I gave her the semen and the Cristal, she caught a flight to Detroit."

As he listened to the details of story, he got a sickening feeling that she may have been telling him the truth. But could his wife have really done this to him. Did she have it in her?

"Anyway, Tamela had the Cristal delivered to your room as soon as she saw you walk through the hotel lobby. And just as I thought, you popped the cork and got your drink on. Minutes later, you were out cold." Toni smiled triumphantly.

That was the reason I ended up knocked out in my room, he thought. That's why Ethan couldn't find him; he had been drugged. Things were starting to make sense to him.

"You being out cold was very important because I couldn't have you roaming around the halls of the hotel for people to see while you're supposed to be in an elevator raping some-one; I had to make sure you didn't have an alibi. So when Ethan came by your room later that evening looking for you, you were out cold, making you a real suspect. Even to him."

Dumbfounded, Calvin stared at his wife. *She did this*, he finally admitted to himself. *She really did this, but why?*

"So what's next," she thought aloud. "Oh yeah, the attack.

193

I arranged for the attack to happen in the elevator because I knew they had security cameras in them. I wanted the entire thing to be caught on tape, so you'll look even guiltier."

After hearing this, Calvin sat down on the edge of the bed. It was either that or fall down. And from what Toni was telling him, he knew it was only a matter of time before he fell on his ass.

She smiled when she noticed he finally took her advice. "I hired Alton—that's the guy who played you in the attack—to meet with Tamela in the elevator at 1:00 A.M. I knew you were out cold by then. You know, he looks a whole hell of a lot like you—same complexion, same build, same pretty black ass.

"But there was one problem—he didn't have that birthmark on his ass like you have. And since his ass was going to star in this video, I had to draw your birthmark on his right ass cheek. Damn! I'm smart.

"Anyway, remember your semen that I gave Tamela before meeting Alton on the elevator . . . she put your semen inside her. That's the reason why your DNA matched the DNA of the semen that the doctors retrieved from the rape kit. But there was one small glitch that could have blown this whole thing out of the water, one thing we didn't consider. And that was the DNA from my saliva. When they created the DNA profile from the semen found inside Tamela, they also picked up the DNA from my saliva. Boy, we were fucked for a little while, but thanks to Tamela's quick thinking, when the detectives questioned her about the female saliva they retrieved from her rape kit, she told the detectives that she was bisexual and that her girlfriend had just performed oral sex on her earlier before she was raped. Boy, did we dodge a bullet with that one!

"Of course, she had to end up explaining this to her boyfriend. Thinking she was bisexual and cheating on him, he took off. But what does she care?—she's three million dollars richer."

Calvin's mouth dropped open in disbelief.

Toni walked over to him, put her index finger on his chin, and pushed upward, closing his mouth for him. "You look like you're catching flies, darling." She took a few steps back from him and smiled.

Calvin just stared her, wondering where in the hell was the woman he married three years ago. Where was his wife? Did he do this to her? Did his infidelities and disrespect turn the angel that he once knew into the evil monster that stood before him, smiling at him as she revealed her diabolical scheme to him. The smug grin on her face let him know that she was genuinely enjoying the anguish she'd put him through.

She continued, "Where was I?—Oh yes, the attack. Now that we had you out cold in your hotel room with no one to corroborate your story that you were sleeping, the stage was now set for some action." She rubbed her hands together in anticipation of revealing the rest of her story as she moved around the room.

"Tamela and Alton got on the elevator together pretending to have a nice conversation and then he got a little out of hand wanting to grope her, and get his freak on with her. But when she resisted, as she was instructed to do, he attacked her." She smiled as she stared at her dumbfounded husband. "He beat the hell outta that poor child and then pretended to rape her. We couldn't actually let him have sex with her, though, because of the DNA and all. You understand, don't you?"

She didn't wait for an answer. "Anyway, later I asked Tamela how was she able to take so many blows from Alton without losing it and she said that every time he hit her, she thought about all the money she was going to get—the things we'll do for money." She laughed.

"You see, Calvin, while everybody is walking around thinking your wife is the dumbest most gullible woman they've ever seen, it really was just an act. I had to play the supportive wife. I had to show the world that I believed my husband was innocent in order for my plan to work. But all this trouble would have been for naught if you decided that you wanted to fight this out with Tamela in court, but I knew you wouldn't. I knew that sooner or later, you were going to crack. I knew Joseph and the record company executives would talk you into offering this girl a settlement, even though you and I both know that you weren't guilty."

She walked over to him, put her hands on her knees, and leaned forward to look into his eyes. "It must have been hell, being accused of a crime that you know that you didn't commit, all the while looking guilty as hell. It must have been hell knowing that the whole world had already tried you and found you guilty of a crime that you didn't commit." She smiled. "But you had me, didn't you, honey? I was the only one who believed in you—me, Antoinette Michelle Wallace, the good wife—I was the only thing you had."

All this time he thought he was the shit, that he was the one running things, and all the while she was the puppet master manipulating the strings and he was the dummy executing her every command.

She stood up, stepped back, and crossed her arms. "Anyway, I knew you'd offer Tamela a settlement, and of course, she was going to take it—that was the plan. The one thing I didn't count on was you raping me. I guess in some twisted roundabout way I deserved it. I had pushed you to the edge. It was after you forced yourself on me that I saw my doctor and started taking birth control pills. I couldn't take the chance of getting pregnant by you, not now, not after me, Tamela, and Alton put in so much work. And it was a good thing I did get on the pill too."

She walked over to the window and looked out at the moving truck that held her belongings. She turned back around and glanced at him. "You started changing on me, going soft, wanting to make love and shit without a condom, wanting to start a family and make a baby. You know that first night that you made love to me without a condom was nice. Real nice. It reminded me of the way things were before you became the famous Blayze. While you were making love to me, I actually thought about chucking this entire plan out of the window and trying to make this work with you, but I realized that it was much too late. Too many other people were involved for me to turn back now."

Calvin shook his head in total disbelief. She played him, and it was all too much for him to digest.

"Now comes the why." She walked back over to where he sat. "Why would I put together such an elaborate scheme?— I'll tell you why. Seven years ago, I met this handsome shy seventeen-year-old who wrote the most beautiful prose that I'd ever read. He was a gifted poet, but he hid his gift away from the world. Knowing that he had the potential to be a star, I encouraged him to share his talent with others, and he did. And as much as he was a wonderful writer, he was an even more gifted lyricist. The world went mad over him, and the man I fell in love with fell in love with the money, fame, and the women. He got caught up and forgot about me. Instead of treating me like the woman he loved, he treated me like I was a piece of shit that he accidentally stepped on while on his way to fuck one of his many groupies. Remember?"

He remembered.

"When I threatened to leave, he threw up in my face the fact that I would leave with nothing. He held that prenuptial agreement over my head constantly, reminding me that the support and love that over the years didn't mean shit. He constantly paraded his ho's around town for everyone to see. He didn't even have the decency to hide his affairs, so I could at least, for the rest of the world, for my mom and my friends, pretend that I had a good man that loved and respected me. And then when I asked for a baby, he laughed at me and swore that I would never bear his seed for fear that I was after his fuckin' money."

She walked over to him with fire in her eyes. She glared down at him. "I helped you earn that money, Calvin. I helped you earn every fuckin' million." She poked him in the chest with her finger. "And you couldn't give me one fuckin' cent. You made me do this; you gave me no other choice. I gave you all of me and took nothing for myself, and you took all of me and gave me nothing but grief and heartache.

"Three months ago, you came home and climbed in bed

with me with the scent of another woman's pussy on your lips. And when I raised a stink about it, your response was, 'Bitch, I just went triple platinum, you oughta be happy I want to fuck you.'"

Damn, he thought. Now he could see what he did to her. He was just that damn cold. He was surprised that he wasn't lying on the floor somewhere with a bullet in his head, compliments of his wife.

Toni stepped back and stared at him as she crossed her arms. "Well, tell me, Calvin—what is triple platinum? Is that when you sell three million copies of your CD? Well, baby, let me tell you something. Remember the settlement that you gave Tamela. That was fifteen million dollars, right? Let's see, Tamela's lawyer took twenty five percent of the settlement, which equals 3.75 million; this left Tamela with 11.25 million. She divided that amount with me and your impersonator, Alton. Which means we each received 3.75 million apiece."

She walked over to the dresser, picked up her purse, and slipped it over her shoulder. "Two hours ago, I checked my bank account online and three million plus was deposited into my new checking account, compliments of Miss Waters—and you, of course." Feeling vindicated, she prepared to bring it all home. She walked over to him, put her hand on her hip, and looked down at him. "So, Calvin, it seems that I am three million dollars richer, and to use your own words, 'bitch, I just went triple platinum,' and I just fucked you."

She laughed and started walking out the bedroom. When she reached the door, she stopped, turned around, and walked back over to where he was still sitting. She leaned over and kissed him softly on the lips. When she was finished, she looked down at him and smiled. "I thought I should at least kiss you, since I just fucked you." With those final words, Toni walked out of the bedroom and headed downstairs.

Still reeling from her confession, Calvin just sat on the edge of the bed not knowing what to do or to say.

"All right, boys, are we straight?" she asked the moving men that were still downstairs waiting for her.

"Yes, ma'am," the man in charge responded. "Everything's packed and ready to go."

"Good." She opened up her purse, rummaged through it for a few seconds, and retrieved a piece of paper and her new apartment keys. "Here is my new address." She handed the mover the slip of paper. After removing one of the keys from the key ring, she slipped it in the palm of his hand. "And here is the key to get in. Please leave the key on the kitchen windowsill when you are finished, and then you'll be done."

"Yes, ma'am." He smiled before gathering up the rest of the men and left.

Toni took in her surroundings for the very last time and then walked out the door. With a smile dancing on her lips, she practically bounced off the stairs of the mansion to her Jaguar. She pulled out her cell phone and dialed Ethan's number. Silently, she prayed that it wasn't too late. A month had passed since she left him standing alone in the hotel room after he declared his love to her. She wondered whether his love for her was still intact or had he offered himself to another.

"Hello."

"Ethan . . . hi, it's me, Toni Wallace."

"Toni?" He was surprised to hear from her since they hadn't spoken in a while. "Is everything okay? Is something wrong with Calvin?"

"No, nothing's wrong." She paused before continuing. "I just left Calvin."

"Really." It was the only thing he could say. Part of him was happy that she'd finally come to her senses and left her husband, but part of him was concerned about what made her finally pack up and leave him. "Are you okay?"

"Yes, yes, I'm fine." She smiled. She was happy that he still cared about her even though she ran off when he confessed his love for her. She hoped that he didn't hate her. "I was just wondering . . . we could maybe get together and talk . . . if you were free."

"Talk? Sure." Ethan smiled and nodded as if she could see him. "That sounds great." He was anxious to see her pretty smile again. "So when do you want to see me?"

"How about right now? I could come by your place. We could have a drink and talk." She hesitated. "We could talk about us."

"About us? That sounds great. I'll guess I'll see you in a few minutes?"

"Yes, I'll be right over."

Calvin suddenly knew what to do and say. He raced down the spiral staircase and out the front door to find Toni, but it was too late. She was already gone.

"Damn," he said as he stood on the steps of his 6.8 million dollar mansion. He pushed his hands through his hair, turned around, and looked at his multi-million dollar home. He thought about the Navigator, H2, and Mercedes that occupied three out of four of his garages. He thought about the custom-built walk-in closet that was stocked wall to wall with the most expensive designer labels and shoes. And he couldn't forget about the ice. The ice that dripped from his wrists, neck, and ears. He had everything that money could buy and more, but for the first time he realized it didn't mean a thing if he didn't have Toni.

He thought about everything that Toni said when she revealed her scheme to him earlier. Although he was furious because of all the shit she put him through in the past three months, he knew that his anguish was nothing compared to the hell he put her through for the past two and a half years. His blatant disregard for her feelings and constant fucking around on her had driven her to this point.

He knew she was right when she said she helped him earn every cent of his millions, but instead of acknowledging her contribution to their fortune, he foolishly dangled that prenuptial agreement over her head. How in the world could he hurt her like that? She had been his strength when he was weak, his sounding board when he needed to vent, and his guide when he got off track, and how did he repay her—by fucking every woman that cocked open her legs for him.

What happened to Calvin, he wondered. What happened to the man that she had married? What happened to that seventeen-year-old that she fell in love with, the one that knew about the value she added to his life? That seventeen-year-old got caught up, caught up in the hype that the world of hip-hop world promoted—fast women, fast money, fast everything—but at what cost? Although his pockets were still swollen, he had nothing without Toni. *Without Toni, all of this don't mean shit!*

"This couldn't be the end," he told himself. He couldn't let Toni walk out of his life forever. Even though she had just taken him to hell and back, he knew she still loved him. He only prayed that his behavior hadn't caused irreversible damage to that love.

Chapter Twenty-one

Toni stood outside the door of Ethan's condominium. She raised her fist to knock then hesitated. Nervously she bit her bottom lip as she thought about the man on the other side of the door. She wondered if the love he'd offered her over a month ago was still available. *He agreed to see me,* she thought. Maybe he was just being polite, or maybe he still had a place in his heart for her.

Then she thought about her role in this get-together. What was she going to say to him? Would she be brave enough to admit that she was in love with him, or would she chicken out and give him some line about her "appreciating his friendship"? She still hadn't made up her mind. She also hadn't completely sold herself on the idea of going through with this meeting, part of her wanting to turn tail and run.

On the other side of the door, Ethan paced the floor and nervously wrung his hands as he anxiously awaited her arrival, his heart pounding with anticipation. He didn't know if it would be good news or bad. Maybe she wanted to tell him that she wanted to be with him, or maybe she was going to tell him that since she left Calvin she would be packing up and moving out of town and would never be able to see him again.

He quickly pushed that thought out of his mind. She wouldn't have contacted him, after not seeing him for over a month, to tell him that she wouldn't be able to see him again . . . unless she was just trying to tie up loose ends before moving out of town.

"No, that's not it." He stopped pacing to fluff a few pillows on his couch in an attempt to busy himself while he waited for her arrival. After rearranging the pillows, he glanced at his watch. He wondered what was taking her so long.

Anxious, he moved over to his front window and looked out, hoping to see some sign that she hadn't stood him up. He immediately spotted her Jaguar parked next to his Lexus. *She is here.* Unable to wait another second, he rushed to the door and opened it.

Startled, Toni looked up to find him staring down at her with a happy but surprised look on his face.

"Toni."

"Hi." She smiled nervously as she lowered her fist that was still poised to knock on the door. "I-um-I—"

He stared down at her. She was more beautiful than he remembered. His first instinct was to grab her and pull her into his arms but he resisted; instead, he stepped back and invited her in.

Toni nervously stepped into the condominium. She turned and looked up at him. "You're looking good," she said, trying to make small talk.

"Well, you look great." He smiled. "Absolutely stunning."

Toni blushed and nervously looked down at the floor.

He slipped his finger under her chin and tilted her head up, forcing her to look at him. "Hey," he said, "you should be used to compliments, Toni. Calvin should have told you how beautiful you are every single minute of every single day since the first day he laid eyes on you."

"Ethan . . ." She blushed even more. She stared up at him, wondering if she was going to go through with it. Was she going to confess her feelings to him? She had made the call to him and the drive over, but that was when she'd just left Calvin; she was feeling braver then. Putting Calvin in his place had given her a feeling of fearlessness. There was nothing she couldn't do. But now that she was standing there in front of Ethan, waiting to tell him that she loved him, all of her bravery went out the window. "You're too kind."

"Damn!" Ethan said, "Where the hell are my manners? Would you like to sit down?"

"Yes," she said as he led her to the sofa. She sat down and looked around the professionally decorated room. This was her first time at his place, and she was impressed with his sense of style and taste.

"Would you like something to drink?"

Even though she knew a drink of something alcoholic would give her some backbone, she declined.

Ethan sat down on the sofa next to her. "So you left Calvin?" He was still curious as to what transpired between them to make her leave him. After being so adamant about standing by his side, the sudden decision to leave him worried him. He hoped Calvin hadn't hurt her physically.

"Yes. I finally did it," she proudly said.

"But why? I mean why after all this time; after all you've been through with him. I thought you would never leave him."

She knew this was coming. Knowing that she could never tell him about her framing Calvin for rape, she had already decided how she would answer it. Her explanation wouldn't be a total lie; it just wouldn't be entirely true. "I thought I'd never leave him too, but I finally woke up. I wanted to make my marriage work. I didn't want to be one of those women who couldn't hold her marriage together. I thought those women didn't know how to love their men, and that if I loved him enough, we could overcome anything."

"But?"

"But it wasn't. Love couldn't save my marriage. Nothing could save my marriage. Calvin and I had two different goals. Mine was to make our marriage work; his was to sleep with every woman he met."

"I'm sorry."

"Don't be. I knew he was unfaithful, but I chose to stay. Then one day, I finally got tired of shouldering my entire marriage by myself. There were two of us in our relationship, but only one of us was doing the work. I realized then that my marriage was a lost cause and I deserved better, so I just packed up and left."

"Good for you." He smiled. "I always knew you deserved better; I'm just glad that you finally realized it too."

"Me too."

"So, how did Calvin take it?"

"He was at a loss for words. I guess he thought I would never leave him. He should be happy now—now he gets to sleep around without any guilt . . . as if he had any." She smiled.

"Yeah. So . . . what are your plans now—now that you're a single woman?"

"Well, I've got a little place not far from here. I'm gonna chill out a little, relax and enjoy life for a change." She thought about the reason for her visit. She was supposed to be revealing her love to him, but instead she was talking about chilling out. She swallowed as she tried to muster up the courage to tell how she felt.

"You mind if I chill out with you sometimes?"

"No, I don't mind. That would be nice." *It's now or never.* "Ethan,"—she swallowed again—"I wanted to talk to you because I have something I wanted to tell you."

He smiled. "I'm hanging on your every word."

She laughed nervously as she felt all her courage drain away. She couldn't tell him. She didn't have the nerve to follow through. Thinking quickly, she went for the friendship speech. "I just wanted to let you know that you have been an incredible friend to me and Calvin—especially me—through this entire ordeal, and that I truly appreciate it. I truly value your presence in my life."

That wasn't what he wanted to hear, but he didn't let his face reveal his disappointment. "Thanks," was all he could say.

"No, I want to thank you for being there for me, for listening to me bitch and moan about my husband, and for not judging me. I'm honored to call you my friend."

"I'm honored to be your friend." He reached over, took her hand, and gave it a gentle squeeze.

Suddenly feeling overwhelmed, Toni glanced at her watch, pretending to check the time. "I really should be going," she said as she gently retrieved her hand and stood up.

Ethan rose to his feet. *So that was it*, Ethan thought. *She just wanted to thank me. She wasn't here to tell me she was moving away and that she could never see me again.* But she also wasn't there to tell him that she loved him. Although he hadn't heard the words that he wanted to hear, he was determined not to give up. He wasn't going to miss this moment to reiterate his love for her.

He thought about their meeting in the hotel room over a month go. He remembered the way she responded to him, the way she responded to his kiss, to his touch. He knew she cared for him, that her feelings for him ran much deeper than a friendship.

He walked her to the door. As she stood there about to say goodbye, he took her hand again and stared into her eyes. "I know you value our friendship, Toni, and so do I. But you do know that I still love you. You do know that I want more than just a friendship from you; I still want to be with you, to love you like no one else can."

She needed to hear that. She needed to know that he still loved her and still wanted her. His words gave her the strength to finally reveal her true feelings for him. "Ethan," she whispered, "I love you too." She felt a warm relief flow over her. She reached up and stroked his face.

As Ethan heard those words come from her lips, he felt an enormous relief. He prayed that he wasn't dreaming, that the woman he fell in love with over a year ago was actually in love with him too.

"You love me too?" He wanted to be sure his ears weren't playing tricks on him.

"Yes, Ethan." She smiled up at him. "I love you too."

With new confidence, he pulled her closer, slowly lowered his head, and covered her lips with his.

She surrendered herself to him as her arms encircled his neck and welcomed him into her arms, into her heart, into her life.

Chapter Twenty-two

Two years later, a very pregnant Toni Michaels smiled to herself as she wobbled out of her gynecologist's office building. She was very happy with Dr. Starke's comments that she and baby were doing fine. Ethan wanted to join her for her final doctor's appointment, but with their baby due any day now, he had too many loose ends to tie up at their record company.

The past two years had taken Toni, Ethan, and Calvin through a very emotional roller-coaster ride. After realizing that the fortune he tried to keep from his wife meant nothing if he didn't have her, Calvin threw away his pride and bad-ass attitude and set out to convince Toni that he was a changed man. He quickly learned that Ethan had already stolen her heart.

Outraged and feeling betrayed by their union, he still fought to get her back, but the damage that his cheating had caused to their marriage and her love for him had proven to be irreversible. Finally admitting defeat, Calvin just took his losses, licked his wounds, and counted it "a lesson learned." He quickly went back into the studio to work on his next two CD's.

Later, he granted Toni the divorce that she requested. Shortly after the divorce was final, Toni and Ethan were married.

A few months later, Toni purchased a small struggling record company with the money she received from framing Calvin and renamed it "Triple Platinum." They signed a few promising new talents including Flawless and Prophetic, two of their most successful lyricists.

Flawless had a clean nice-guy image about him. He was married with two kids and rapped about thought-provoking socially conscious issues, whereas Prophetic was his complete opposite. Prophetic reminded Toni of Calvin—he thrived on being a bad boy, and the world loved him.

With these two promising rhyme masters on their label and Ethan's expertise and contacts, they managed to turn things around at Triple Platinum. Ethan never asked Toni where she got all the money from to buy the record company. He assumed it was part of her divorce settlement, and she didn't tell him otherwise.

Toni half-expected Calvin to try to blow the whistle on her and her two accomplices, but he never did. She also knew that he would never be able to convince anyone that his sweet and demure wife could ever come up with such an outrageous and diabolical scheme.

After starting the car and pulling into traffic, Toni turned up the radio to listen to the "Top Four at Four" as she headed back to the office to see her husband. (They had plans to see a movie later that evening.) She listened as the

DJ announced the single that was holding the number two spot on the countdown:

"Dropping down to the number two spot after holding on to number one for six weeks in a row, is the bad boy himself, Blayze, with 'It Ain't Over'."

Toni smiled as she listened to her ex-husband's song.

The record executives at Southern Scope were right—we are a forgiving society. After Tamela dropped the rape charges against Calvin, he went right back to work and won back his fans' hearts and wallets by putting out the hottest and "dopest" rhymes ever written. He was gifted, and no one could deny it. His fans rushed right back out to the record stores and concert halls to show their forgiving spirit and ongoing support, pushing him back to the number one spot, where he reigned supreme.

That was until Triple Platinum, Toni's new record company, released the first single from Prophetic. The nineteen-year-old rap sensation proved to be Calvin's biggest competition. According to the latest issue of *Flow* magazine, he was "a force to be reckoned with." With his debut CD about to drop the following month, she knew that her ex-husband would no longer be the reigning king of hip-hop. Prophetic was about to hand him his ass on a platter.

After Calvin's song finished, the DJ announced the single that had knocked his song down one spot:

"Taking the number one spot as the most requested song of the day is newcomer, Prophetic, with 'Face Down'."

Toni smiled to herself when she realized that her new artist had stolen the number one spot on the countdown from her ex-husband. Prophetic was going to blow up, and she and Ethan knew it. She only hoped that her new up-and-coming star wouldn't let the fame go to his head the way Calvin let it go to his.